## Praise for Christopher Meeks's
## The Middle-Aged Man and the Sea
## and Other Stories:

"A collection that is so stunning...that I could not help but move on to the next story."
— Entertainment Weekly

"Poignant and wise, sympathetic to the everyday struggles these characters face."
— Los Angeles Times

"These are original, articulate, engaging stories which examine life in America from the unique perspectives of ordinary people searching for their share of the promises held out as part of the American dream. ... The *Middle-Aged Man and The Sea* is highly recommended, highly entertaining, highly rewarding reading."
— The Midwest Book Review

"Christopher Meeks bounces onto the literary scene as a vibrant new voice filled with talent and imagination. The *Middle-Aged Man and the Sea* is one of the finer collections of short stories that will rapidly rise to the top to of the heap of a battery of fine writers of this difficult medium."
— Grady Harp, Top Ten Reviewer, Amazon.com

"Mr. Meeks has a wonderfully fun writing style—witty, cynical, and often poignant. His stories are about the stuff of life: love and heartbreak, sickness and death, desires and struggles, spirituality and the search for meaning."
— Janet Rubin, Novel Reviews

"In this collection of short stories, Christopher Meeks examines the small heartbreaks and quiet despair that are so much a part of all of our lives. He does it in language that is resonant, poetic, and precise. Franz Kafka said that a book should be an ice-axe to break the frozen sea within us. This collection is just such a weapon. If you like Raymond Carver, you'll love Meeks. He may be as good—or better. He deserves major recognition."
— author David Scott Milton, *Paradise Road*

"If the publishing and reading world is fair and just, Christopher Meeks is destined to be widely read and deservedly honored."
— Carolyn Howard-Johnson, Myshelf.com

"Many of these tales have appeared in American literary journals, but reading them together, you get the full impact of Meeks's talent, as he takes you in a head-long assault through ordinary day-to-day life, the mundane under the microscope and given the once-over through Meeks's careful eye."
— Susan Tomaselli, Dogmatika

# Acclaim for Christopher Meeks's Months and Seasons and Other Stories:

"The stories in *Months and Seasons* are like potato chips: you can't read just one. Just a few sentences into the first piece, "Dracula Slinks into the Night," I immediately felt at home in the world Meeks has created."
— Marc Schuster, Small Press Reviews

"For those readers fortunate enough to have read Christopher Meeks's first short story collection, The *Middle-Aged Man and the Sea*, and discovered the idiosyncrasies of Meeks's writing style and content, rest assured that this new collection, *Months and Seasons*, not only will not disappoint, but also it will provide further proof that we have a superior writer of the genre in our presence."
— Grady Harp, Top Ten Reviewer, Amazon.com

"With this collection, Christopher Meeks proves there is an audience for short stories. His characters are well defined with problems that they can't resolve. There are twelve tales that reveal a lot about our present society. Meeks's stories reminded me of those of John Cheever."
— Gary Roen, The Midwest Book Review

"Full of complete randomness and quirkiness, ingredients I cherish, the stories in this twelve-story collection chronicle the eccentricities of an array of diverse characters, who are dealing with life thrown at them in the only way actually possible: by dealing with their problems, not escaping them."
— Rachel Durfor, Rebecca's Reads

# Other Books by Christopher Meeks

*Months and Seasons and Other Stories*

*Who Lives?* (A Drama)

*The Brightest Moon of the Century* (A Novel)

# The Middle-Aged Man
# & The Sea

*Stories by Christopher Meeks*

White Whisker Books
Los Angeles

ISBN 978-0-615-24917-9
Library of Congress Control Number: 2005908573
Copyright © 2005 by Christopher Meeks
First Edition

Library of Congress Cataloging-in-Publication Data

Meeks, Christopher.
    The middle-aged man and the sea / by Christopher Meeks – 1st ed.
        p. cm.
1. United States – Social life and customs – 21st century—Fiction.
PS3613.E374 M53 2005
813.6

*Cover photo:* Neil Bromfield for Blink Creative. *Typeface:* Electra

*Editor*, Nomi Isak Kleinmuntz

*Book Design*, Daniel Will-Harris, www.will-harris.com

White Whisker Books, Los Angeles

*Dedicated to my mother, Sidney Wear,*
*who has encouraged me in writing short stories,*
*and also dedicated to the late Stanley Fuchs,*
*one of the country's great restaurateurs.*

# Contents

"Divining" first appeared in the *Santa Barbara Review* and was reprinted in *Rosebud*.

"Engaging Ben" first appeared in *Writers' Forum*.

"Academy Award Afternoon and Evening" first appeared in the *Clackamas Literary Review* and was reprinted in *Rosebud*.

"He's Home" first appeared in the *Midday Moon*.

"Shooting Funerals" first appeared in *The Southern California Anthology*.

"Green River" first appeared in the *Midday Moon* and was reprinted in *Rosebud*.

"Dear Ma" first appeared in the *Clackamas Literary Review*.

"The Scent" first appeared in *Rosebud*.

"The Middle-Aged Man and the Sea" first appeared in *Rosebud*.

# Academy Award Afternoon & Evening

L ila and Dave have us over for the Academy Awards, a mini-party to use their big-screen TV one last time before they sell the thing. The monster set doesn't fit their newly remodeled living room, which has new oak wood floors. Blond flooring vs. a walnut cabinet is the deal. I've been feeling disconnected lately, what with taking on too many freelance assignments that explain the God-damn computer of all things—keeps me up too many nights with bad coffee—who reads these things anyway?—so the point is I can use a good party.

My wife and I show up at four, and the first thing I notice is the new Mercedes in the driveway. It looks like an ad: silver body, chrome wheels, moon roof, sparkling on the red brick driveway under a sun that also shines across town on movie stars and next to a lawn so perfect and green you want to open up his trunk, pull out a golf club, and hit a ball so hard and imperfectly it leaves a divot the size of Texas on what otherwise is an emerald carpet. I know for a fact he keeps the grass so lush thanks to an automated sprinkler system that senses when the turf is thirsty, and valves open and probably spray Perrier onto each perfect pixel before anything is able to choke or strangle or die. My system is that when my lawn is brown and gasping and seeing mirages of Turf Builder, I hope and pray that a good hosing will help.

We enter the house, admire the remodeled living room, its inlaid oak floor, the built-in bookshelves, and the ergonomic Herman Miller chairs. A marketing man, Dave smiles and nods, being the friendly, unassuming guy he is. He wears a pastel Polo shirt that matches the walls and betrays the fact he's followed through on his New Year's resolution to get in shape. He hits the gym each morning at 5:30 when more sensible souls like me are sleeping. His belly is flat. "So you like it," he says, his arm wavering over the living room like Vanna White pointing to a Porsche.

"Yes, beautiful," says my wife, gathering reconstruction ideas in her eyes, making me wonder how many more articles I'll need to write. "Great," I say, noticing Lila in the kitchen, dark, a mere smudge in the background. As we approach the counter that divides the two rooms, I see Lila wears a baggy, gray sweatshirt that gives little sense to her form, as if she is out of focus. I then notice her uncharacteristic frown.

"Hey," I say, and she smiles bright like a snapshot of snow and yanks off the plastic wrap to a Gelson's hors d'oeuvre platter of shrimp, cheese log, crackers, and liver paste and offers me a taste.

"You're just in time," she says, "They're still arriving." She points to a small screen TV in the kitchen. Little bitty movie stars wave. Lila lifts a remote control and aims it into the living room like Luke Skywalker with a laser sword. The large screen leaps to life, basso profundo, showing the red carpet canyon leading into the Shrine Auditorium with columns of Oscars bigger than Buicks. Hillary Swank in an olive gown, a chandelier of jewelry, and all those teeth, hugs her husband Chad Lowe and says that "the role afforded me an understanding of humanity." I wish I had that. An understanding. I'm in the dark. Salma Hayek sweeps in with pink diamonds and deep cleavage—actual size on the big screen—

and she hopes Pedro will win that night. Roger Ebert, a blimp in black, just grins. I'm with him. Being married for fifteen years, I don't see many naked breasts anymore.

The four of us sit on the sofa and talk. The platter goes around. Dave pours margaritas into martini glasses. We look elegant, get a little silly, glance occasionally to the movie stars inside the auditorium—Nicole Kidman in a backless gold gown, Faye Dunaway in white, and perfect Jack Nicholson gets away with sunglasses in the front row.

"We ought to drive to Mexico together sometime," says Dave.

"Sure, why not?" I say, thinking at this point I'd better get another credit card. "Let's go in your Mercedes," I add.

He laughs and says, "I'd love to drive. Have you driven a Benz? It handles better than a BMW." He says we'll go to La Fonda and eat steak and lobster on the shore, drink mescal and think of our youth. I realize our youth, like these margaritas, has fled.

As we eat the ideal salad from a crystal bowl, the tomatoes red, cubed, and flavorful—several staining my tan pants—this is around two hours in during the Best Short Documentary Award and with some guy in a wheel chair—I look to Lila and thank her. You can never thank anyone enough. She stares at me seriously. Am I frowning? I hope not. Lila says, "So if a Mack Truck hit you right now, what would you say to this all?"

"Ouch," says my wife, and we laugh.

"I'll sue you," says Dave and we burst out again.

"What the fuck are we here for?" I utter. No laughter. "Why?" I ask. "Why ask about this all?"

"Oh, well, my mom died last night." The words come out as if she were ashamed. She didn't mean to ruin the party. The big screen TV, which does not seem so big now, is mute. "She's been sick and out of it for a while," says Lila. There's an awkward pause at the Academy, as if they're trying to find the script. Billy Crystal, the host, stares directly at us. Lila says, "She finally gave in last night."

"Good ol' Dorothy," adds Dave, raising his empty margarita.

We raise our glasses and sip nothing. I didn't know Dorothy was her mother's name. I don't really know Lila at all, I realize, but I do know that a mother's a mother. Lila is a mother. Their little boy, age seven, is back in his bedroom playing Nintendo. He's been doing so all night, out of sight, and I now hear the distant sounds of bombs dropping and jet fighters crashing. What else do I know about Lila? She is the wife of Dave and does something or other at the Rand Corporation. It's a think tank, as they say, so she must think for them. What does she think? What do you say?

"I'm sorry," says my wife. That's a good thing to say, and I echo it. Lila stares out blankly. Dave says nothing. I hear the sprinklers turn on.

# Green River

We escaped Merri's mother's place in Denver at one p.m. and made it as far as Green River, Utah, the halfway point to Los Angeles, before the road was too much of a blur to continue further. We found Green River a stubby oasis in a vast, high desert, west of the Rockies, in the parched nothingness known only for its dinosaur bones.

There's a green river in Green River, and when we arrived and checked into the waterside, peach-colored motel, the summer sun was setting just over the wide but slowly flowing confluence, making me think of the last pulse of my own arteries. One day, you're young, laughing, eating Cheetos, the next, you're locked in a car with your wife and 11-year-old son, no one talking to each other, the acidity of anger drip drip dripping at your insides if not your wife's.

At ten p.m., tired of the cable TV, son Harry wanted candy. Merri was in the bathroom, secluded. "Sure," I said, reading the local paper, seeing who had won the local cow chip-tossing contest, "Let's get some candy. The sugar rush might do us good." Overhearing, Merri said take our time in a tone that implied to me, "Drop dead." Hell, she'd been the one to suggest we drive to Colorado so she could help her mother recover from hip surgery. I had asked what would Harry and I do there? She had said it'd be a fun family thing, that my accounting firm owed me a week's vacation, and in

Denver there's fun stuff, the mountains, the new aquarium, the zoo. We could do that while she communed with Mom.

Maybe I had misunderstood her. Then again, we had been tense for months in the way the very structure of pota- toes, mail, and "your shoes" changes with the insertion of "damn." Merri resented Denver—said she was trapped with her demanding mother while we were off at the aquarium, the zoo, hiking, having fun, etc., etc. I had gotten as far as saying, "But this is what you wanted," when she banged the silverware around and said she wanted a divorce. I'd told her to grow up. She then gave me the finger and slammed the dishwasher shut. I smashed my hand down on the Formica counter, and she lunged at me, her hands in strangled fists, ready to hit. I grabbed her wrists to hold her. After we both struggled, and I saw the serious, deeply creased, and hateful look on her face—and imagined mine—for some reason I laughed. "We're living in a sitcom," I said. "Any moment we'll get to the H.E.—the humorous epilogue." She pulled back. Days later, we still hadn't reached the H.E. If our ten- sions were guitar strings, we could play, "Cry Me a Green River."

Anyway, now that we were here in Utah, candyless, Harry and I hopped in the car and drove across the Green River bridge to the truck stop on the other side. I parked by the front door of the mini-mart, not needing gas, and we beetled our way inside. Harry selected a Nutrageous candy bar, even though I told him the Salted Nut Roll was better. When he didn't take my sage advice, I bought both bars to prove my claim.

Outside in the evening's air and under the fluorescent canopy, we traded bits of each other's bars to compare. The full moon was just coming up over the trees alongside the river. Crickets chirped, a gentle wind caressed our faces, and it was the best blessed moment of the whole trip. "See," I said to Harry. "Be happy for the small things." Beyond the trees lay the desert and the silhouette of scrub. Time and weather had eroded everything to sand and ash.

I chewed a bite of the Nutrageous. So did Harry. The peanuts, caramel, chocolate, and Harry's look of concentration reminded me of when candy bars were all that mattered. We next bit into chunks of the Salted Nut Roll—peanuts, caramel, and some mysterious white center that Harry wanted to know more about. I told him the center's secret— always secret. Did it have spun sugar? he asked. Probably, but who knows how to spin sugar? Rumplestilskin? We ate. In a few minutes, we would have to return to the motel.

As Harry and I chewed like cattle eating cud, I noticed across the way that a good-looking, long-haired woman, early thirties in white shorts, was bending down the full-length of her long tanned legs, touching her pink painted toes on her sandaled feet. She was limber enough and beautiful enough to be on a morning exercise show. She stood next to her green minivan, which was being gassed. A family car. Bend and stretch. I could see she wore a black tube top beneath a loose-fitting green shirt. She did a variety of moves, and one, the way she turned her head and her hair swung around her shoulders, made me flash on Merri in one of our more carefree days: Merri naked with me in a tent on the Kern River, the two of us like loons, laughing. This woman, however, had been sitting for hours, I guessed, and, by the dread of her looking at her watch, she probably would be sitting for a few more. After her exercises, she looked toward the mini-mart's doors. As she walked past us and inside, I noticed her face more. I could see sadness. Did I perceive correctly?

We finished eating our treats—Harry declaring the Nutrageous the winner—and I decided because we were there, I'd get some gas, too. The open bay was on the other side of the woman's minivan. As I filled her up, Harry wanted another candy bar "for the road." Where did he get these lines? "You shouldn't watch so much TV," I said. I gave him money, and as he went in, the long-haired woman came out alone, ashen, looking as if each step was towards her death.

Harry was taking his time, so I went in to retrieve him. As we exited, the woman, leaning against the van, glanced at me. Her eyes reflected what would be, at any moment, tears. I then realized her attention was really on her husband, who was leaving the mini-mart behind me. He was a gentle, husky man her age with short, blond hair. On his back in a carrier was a baby dressed in pink, and another little girl, maybe three, held his hand. He loaded his children into their car seats in the vehicle while I finished gassing and waited for the pump to print my receipt.

The woman moved slowly into the passenger's side. From my angle, she carried her head very low, as if crying quietly. I couldn't help but look into their van as I replaced the hose. She sat next to the man with her chin near her chest. The children in the back were quiet. He was gently telling her something, but she was leaning forward, keeping her head tipped as if gravity had won. The image of utter sadness tore at my stomach. My emotional response surprised me. After all, these were strangers, and I knew nothing of their problems.

I wondered if Merri and I had echoed our silences so loudly at gas stations. Maybe we could press push-pins into a map to chart our gas stops of despair. I continued to watch. He did not react in anger or tell her to grow up. Neither did he place his hand on her back or console her physically. He simply sat there, not looking at her, and spoke soft words to the windshield that I could not hear. She probably blamed him for her lousy life, and there was not a damn thing he could do.

At this point, Harry was extolling the virtues of Nutrageous over the Salted Nut Bar again, and he earnestly asked me if I thought my chocolate was really better. I realized in that moment, as I looked over at the van and saw a ghostly reflection of me inside my own windshield, that no matter how much hope you have, it cannot weave happiness. I touched Harry's shoulder and told him as far as candy bars were concerned, go with your own impressions. Do what you have to do.

# The Middle-Aged Man And The Sea

B ert was a quiet New Yorker, and I, an outgoing Minneso-
tan—both terms, oxymorons. Under normal circum-
stances, we'd never be friends. His idea of a good time was a
serene riverbank and a lot of fishing tackle. Mine: crank up
Bruce Springsteen and give me an air guitar. He lived in Florida, a respected contractor, and I, in California, a stockbroker
with a phone and advice that never stopped. We broke bread
together, though, because we shared the same in-laws, which
was to say, we had married sisters. Once a year at a family
reunion on one coast or another, we'd see each other and bet
which two of four sisters—our wives and their two siblings—
would get into a fight that would be the end of the world. It
was great sport. One wife or another would poke her head
into the porch where the male members were laughing and
smoking cigars and say to her husband, "We're leaving this
instant!" This was as sure as the moon rising, as sure as the
hugs and kisses the sisters gave each other the first few days
and the last.

Eddie, my father-in-law, who ran a steakhouse but looked
like he could run the country, would excuse himself and in

minutes solve the dilemma. He would somehow make it plain that one of his daughters didn't really mean the other's five-year-old was spoiled or that one husband was better than another. How thirty- and forty-year-old women could revert to childhood so easily, I never figured out, but Eddie could fix it. Once he died—an unlucky thing with a golf club on the golf course with Bert during a Florida electrical storm—there were no more family reunions.

Thus I was surprised when Bert called me on a Friday just as the market was closing—at 12:50 p.m. Pacific Daylight Time to be precise or 3:50 his time. He asked if I'd like to go deep-sea fishing in a month. "You know I don't fish, Bert," I said, glancing at my screen, torn between my duties and my brother-in-law. This just wasn't the time for a chat. Not sensing my tension, he told me it's not the fishing that was important, but the time together. The word "time" only reminded me how I was juggling it at this moment.

"The sisters and our kids need to see each other," said Bert.

"I'd love to come, but—"

"Everything's supplied! Beer, food, licenses, rods, bait, and suntan lotion. We'll fish off the coast where rockets take off and astronauts discover the blackness of space."

Bert wasn't known for loquaciousness, so this made me pause, turn away from the screen. I could see I was going to miss the market close anyway, so I may as well focus on why Bert was so eager.

"I thought your neighbor was your good fishing buddy," I said.

"He is. This just seemed like a good reason to bring you out. Haven't seen you for a while."

"I'm not sure what Heather has planned." What I didn't say is that we'd been fighting lately over stupid things. She said I wrinkled the sheets too much, for instance, and that she hated the way Aaron and I could burp-talk to each other. She said what kind of example was I setting for an eight-year-old? I didn't exactly relish the idea of traveling with Heather right now.

As if sensing that, Bert said, "The great thing about fishing is you're away from the family all day. It gives you time to think. I want you to learn how great it is."

"You mean there's more to fishing than slimy bait?"

"Absolutely."

"What the heck," I said. "Live dangerously. I'm sure Heather will leap at the chance to see you all, too."

He was so happy, and after expressing "Wonderful! Wonderful!", he even asked about starting some long-term investments, something he had never warmed to before. I no longer worried about the market closing, but rather, I sold him on buying into a good mutual fund, which he and his wife could add to monthly. That pleased him. In the next few days, not only did I send him the paperwork, but also I made arrangements for Heather, Aaron, and me to travel to Florida.

The next month, with the sisters and kids preparing for a day at the beach, Bert and I took off just after eleven in the morning near Cape Canaveral on a group fishing vessel called the Fortune, which looked like a beaten and rusted toy expanded to a 70-foot length. Captain Abe, bleary-eyed with a stained white cap, had welcomed us on board and said to help ourselves to Bud from a keg in the center cabin. The man had an uncanny resemblance to Skipper from *Gilligan's Island*, though much more wrinkly, weathered and beleaguered. Once out on the bay, the Fortune listed to one side like a drunk's shoe, and my doubts about the inherent fun of this grew. The captain made an announcement to say he'd be cooking cheeseburgers once we were anchored. The food on this luxury voyage also included chips. Bert, who had grown a big bushy beard like Papa Hemingway since the last time I saw him, patted my back and said sometimes things are just an adventure. I noted the sky was dark, electrical looking, but Bert assured me the rods were fiberglass and a poor conductor of electricity.

The boat held sixty rods and fifty men, old men, Florida retiree men—no women. We were a floating male senior citizens center, and Bert and I were its youngest members. I wondered if the little ship carried shock paddles in case one of the men needed resuscitation from so much fun or food. Once anchored at sea, everyone found a seat on either the up side or the down side of the boat. I nudged us toward the up side, as that would be the last part of the boat to sink if it should go under. When Bert went to the bathroom—the "head" as I heard others call it—two kids with buckets passed out small, dead fish parts including things with tentacles. In no time, rods extended and lines dropped down, all rods except mine. I was stuck with what looked like a part from open-heart surgery in one hand and a hook in the other. How did fish know this was something good to eat?

"What are we catching anyway? Sailfish?" I asked the man next to me, who looked like my old pharmacist before he was run over by a bus.

The man laughed, which turned into a wheeze then a cough and headed toward arrhythmia. When he started turning red, I hit him on the back a few times with the force I used for my temperamental blender, which allowed him to laugh again. "Sailfish fishing is a whole other sport," he said, "Bigger rods, bigger line, bigger boat."

"You know what they say about fishing rods and men," I said, "A big rod means a big, you know."

"Really?" he said, taking me seriously.

"Yeah, a big foot," which got him laughing again so hard, I thought I'd kill him yet.

Finally he smiled and said, "We're just going after twenty- to thirty-pounders about 90-feet down." It was the first time I heard weight given as a species. A minute later he shouted and pulled out a fish that at first was a red blur for all the flapping around. The man bashed the creature hard against the gray walkway several times until the fish stopped moving. The bloated thing looked like a dead fish from Mars; its lips weren't thin Cher lips (before she got the collagen injections) but big Mick Jagger lips made ugly as if the fish had been kissing razor blades. It had strange nodules on its sides and what looked like extra fins. Did this fish live next to a nuclear reactor? The man pulled out a pocketknife, jabbed it into the fish's side, and air blurted out, stale dark-sea air that stank like something from the Gorton's or Mrs. Paul's fish factory. The fish deflated. I threw my fish part overboard, unhooked.

The man must have seen my expression because he said, "When you bring these fish up so fast from the deep, they don't have a chance to depressurize, so they expand."

Bert returned and looked a little pasty, probably as pasty as me, and in that moment, I shivered. Perhaps it was the sea breeze that caught me wrong and gave me a chill. I wondered if Bert were seasick. "You okay?" I asked.

"I've been having this stomach thing," he said, and he pulled out a Tagamet, unleashed it from its foil, and chewed the chalky substance. "No problem," he said. "Didn't you get any bait?"

"I was waiting for you," I replied.

He had brought his own rod, a red, shiny instrument that looked well tended. Choosing from an array of hooks on his vest, he picked the largest, and he sharpened it with a file that had jutted from one of his many vest pockets. Every sport has its clothing. I was outfitted more like a bowler.

After hailing a bucket boy, Bert loaded both our hooks with slimy fish parts. We then put our rods over the side and let the lines drop. We didn't speak for a while, and the chatter from the old men was like the soothing mumbles from an audience before a performance. With that and the rhythm of the boat going up and down, the water lapping against the side, the birds circling overhead, and a gentle warm wind passing across my face, I didn't feel the pressure to talk. I could see why people enjoyed this. It sure beat cold calling.

After a while I said, "So how's it going with Janice?" I knew from my wife that he and Janice had had their problems. In fact, he had told me at our father-in-law's funeral that he had planned to divorce Janice until she, the youngest of the sisters, became pregnant against his wishes. "She stopped using birth control and didn't tell me," he had said, adding that he would wait at least twelve years until the newly born Michael was old enough to handle a divorce. That was three years ago. That same weekend all of the brothers-in-law had commiserated about having highly opinionated (read "argumentative") wives, wondering what had happened in the women's upbringing that had made them so resistant to compromise (read "inflexible, stubborn, ornery"). Ah, but the women had passion, and we had been moths to their flames. "Things are surprisingly good now," he said. "Michael's in daycare, which he loves, Annie's in junior high and sailboarding—she might even qualify for the Olympics, did you hear? And Janice is a lot more attentive. We make love like bunnies, and we can talk now."

Love is a strange thing, I thought, as alien as these creatures everyone but us seemed to be hooking. How odd that Janice and Bert were happy, and Heather and I weren't. Why was Heather so critical of me lately? Why didn't she like what I did with the cat food can tops? And why was I so unfulfilled with my job? Maybe I just had to hang in there. Let a few years go by. Somehow I'd sail through this phase of life. After all, the next decade was the stylishly stable gray-haired-at-the-temples fifties and Caribbean cruises. This is to say I was lost, but what the hell, I'd fish.

Bert said we might catch cobia, snook, tarpon, or tripletail—things I'd never heard of or seen on a menu. Why would we want to catch such things? The pharmacist doppelganger next to me caught another blur, a grouper, Bert said.

Bert yanked hard on his line. He had something, too, and as he pulled it onboard, he shouted, "Giant redfish!" He was happy—happier than I'd ever seen him. Happily married allowed for such things. "Thirty pounds at least," said the man next to him. Bert gleamed. Somehow he had the secret, not just of fishing, but of life.

He stepped on the fish gently with his foot instead of beating it to death, and the fish kissed the sky, which is to say it was suffocating in the alien air. The hook was caught in the corner of its mouth—must have hurt like hell. Bert gently worked the hook out as delicately as the doctor who once removed a splinter from my son's five-year-old foot. I was wondering if Bert might pull out a hypodermic needle and give it a euthanasic injection—the compassionate fisherman. When I saw him slide his pocketknife out, however, I figured this was the brutal part. Rather than using the blade, however, he opened his awl, the ice pick-looking thing, the one option I never found a use for when I was a camper as a kid. He pushed it hard into the sea creature's side, creating a small hole where air again whooshed out. The fish flopped harder, and Bert picked it up, held it over the side of the boat, and let it go. The fish took the most beautiful dive, worthy of a slow-motion *Wild Kingdom* segment before a bear would snatch it from the air and eat it. I watched it swim away.

"It'll live?" I asked.

"Yeah, I never keep them. I just like to catch them. My game with destiny."

I nodded as if I knew what that meant. "What about the hole in its side?"

"Fish get the bends, too. Now it'll be okay."

The boat shifted, and our seats came into the sun. A few minutes later Bert said, "I'm dying."

"The sun feels kind of good," I said.

"No, I'm dying. Stomach and colon cancer."

"Is this a joke?"

"Last month, before I called you," he said," I'd gone to the doctor with my stomach thing. X-rays showed a blockage. Doc said it was probably benign, but he wanted to get it out right away, and when he went in, he saw cancer was all over the place."

I was speechless. I was suffocating. "I didn't hear about this!"

"Janice's mother and my parents know, but I wanted to tell you in this way because, you know, I didn't have any brothers. You're the nearest thing to a brother."

"I'm honored, but..." I couldn't look at him. "What about chemo?"

"The cancer's too advanced. Chemo wouldn't do enough other than ruin the remaining quality of life."

"Did you get a second opinion?"

"I've had three. One was more willing to be aggressive and use radiation and chemo, but said, yeah, it'd probably just do me in sooner."

"What about non-traditional? One of my clients said his wife had beaten cancer by bathing with rattlesnake root and eating only chicken."

"This is the South. I eat plenty of chicken."

I was getting light-headed, dizzy, and the motion of the boat didn't help. "How long do you have?"

"Six months of a relatively normal life maybe, then it should happen fast."

Bert had just turned forty-one. This didn't make sense. He looked perfectly fine. "So what're you doing out here fishing with me? Shouldn't you be climbing Mount Shasta or something? Scuba diving? Racing cars?"

He smiled patiently, as if he had all the time in the world to explain it to me. For the next two hours, after my dizziness disappeared, and Bert urging me to eat, he told me how he wanted to live as normal and mundane a life as possible. He had dissolved his construction business and was living jobless on credit cards—his wife's idea. His wife would pay off the cards once he died and received the insurance money. His typical day included doing the grocery shopping, picking up Michael from his camp, and dropping off Annie at her sailboarding lessons.

"I like doing the mundane things because it gives the kids a sense of normalcy. See, it's not me I'm worried about. I worry that my children will be hurt and maybe can't cope for a while. I'm sad they'll be sad."

He was also being practical. He had wallpapered two bedrooms, painted the house inside and out, and taken the cars in for servicing. Annie recently freaked out, he said, about how to buy a car after he was gone, so they went and bought a new one, a black Dodge Dakota, a sports utility vehicle, even though she wouldn't otherwise need a new car for a few years. I imagined him negotiating with the dealer, playing the walking-out game and the salesperson saying wait, he'd check with his manager. Wait. And his heartbeats were used up in a showroom.

"Janice will have to pay bills on her own, though, and to get her better at it, I bought her Quicken."

He said next week he might be back in the hospital to have a colostomy bag installed. His bladder was starting to have problems. In fact, the day before we arrived, doctors installed rubber tubing inside his urethra from his bladder to his penis, as a tumor was pinching off his urethra. When he peed now, he said, he farted at the same time, a "funny short circuit," as he called it.

"Surprising to me, I'm not scared. Angry, yes, sometimes. I think if only I had eaten better or stopped smoking sooner, but you know, this may be some completely random thing. Chance is a part of us. The fact we fell in love with sisters is just hit and miss. There was no destiny that we were to have family reunions. There was no destiny that Eddie would be killed by lightning—it's all random. In a way I feel like I'm moving to a different kind of energy, like I'm one person in one body being separated from randomness, and I'm joining something big and connected and orderly." He laughed. "God, I'm sounding like a Californian now."

I took it as a compliment. As we sat silently for a few moments, I understood better why Janice was so attentive now. This was real. She was losing her husband. She would be a widow, not yet forty.

"It's not like I want to die now," he said.

As he spoke, the words "one fine morning" came to me. One fine morning, what? It occurred to me that at our best moments, on our fine mornings, our future is golden. "Soon" we will buy the right IPO and get rich on stock. "Soon" our spouse will recognize how brilliant we are. "Soon" our lives would make sense. Year-by-year, though, we have less future, and the current always is against us. If we can't be golden or can't be recognized or can't find sense this year, when? Or how? I wish I knew. Bert looked unusually content, as if he knew but couldn't explain. Maybe, I surmised, only when you are dying do you know what is truly valuable.

Bert asked me if I understood the colon. "It absorbs the nutrients from what we eat," he said, and as his colon became more inefficient, he would get less sustenance. In addition, as his doctors told him, he'd become anemic and weak because the cancer itself created such deep nutritional demands that his body would take protein from his muscles, and he would waste away, become thinner and thinner until, he imagined, an IV would have to "feed" him. What would get him first—starvation, the cancer spreading to his liver or other organs, or plain old blockage? Time would tell.

I'd love to say we hugged or cried together or said some amazing words, but we didn't. We passed near the Kennedy Space Center and Bert explained that the area had been selected for shooting up America's rockets because of physics. The closer to the equator you were, the more you took advantage of the earth's rotation, a natural slingshot. Things ascended more easily.

After we were talked out and the schooner was moving in toward the shore, the captain appeared. He thanked us for choosing his boat, apologized for the starboard engine going out, and hoped we would come again. The flag above him waved in the wind. A bird flew by. I held my breath. Bert's watch said 3:50.

# The Scent

A man smelled something odd nearby. The odor was sharp, worse than a dead fish slithering with maggots. No matter which way he turned, and wherever he went, the scent followed.

"I don't smell anything," said Ziva, his wife, who looked at him as if he were going to give her trouble again. "Maybe you should go back to your doctor."

"This has nothing to do with my liver," he replied.

"Then see a shrink," she said.

Their son, Ben, ten, said that the house always smelled badly, like old socks on an aged undertaker. He must have heard it on a TV show—what does he know of undertakers? Their teenage daughter, Judith (no longer Judy), simply said, "Oh, Dad," as if smell were a choice like selecting the kind of clothes he did for himself that embarrassed her—gray sweaters, wing-tip shoes. He was too conservative for his daughter—too boring for his wife, too old for his son.

The man bathed himself twice each day, once before and once after work. He was the bookkeeper at Monty's Carpet World. Even there, among the giant bolts of new and untrammeled berber, Olefin loop, and Monsanto Wear Dated II nylon, he would be jolted with the scent of decay. Nobody showed any response to indicate he or she, too, smelled it. He went to his doctor when he could no longer sleep. The pulsing odor kept him awake.

"Why can't I smell something better, like jasmine?" he told his old friend, Dr. Feinberg.

"Jasmine doesn't bloom this time of year," said the doctor.

"Then how about burnt motor oil? Anything is better than what I'm smelling!"

He was sent to specialists. They would "ah," and nod, as if he were an interesting new piece of the Dead Sea scrolls. X-rays, MRIs, neurological tests, and he came out clean. "Has it diminished at all?" one asked.

"Yes," he said, lying. He wanted no more tests. He thought, perhaps, the smell was something to do with his attitude. He needed a fresher outlook. A voice in his sleep that night told him to fight. Fight what? His family? Fight for a better attitude? Thus, he tried picturing orange poppies—a field of them before an emerald city where he would be heralded as the head of the household. And could they make the place smell like night blooming jasmine?

Do not look at the man behind the curtain.

While he was in the shower reaching for the curtain, a pain shot into his back like a hot electric charge. His teeth clenched, his back arched, and he crumpled. He could hardly breathe, and he surely would faint as the spray hammered like tiny needles onto his naked skin. And the aroma, now musty like a busted sewer pipe in the basement, filled his nose. All he saw was white until a woman, her face as pale as flour, nodded as if she knew the secret of the pursuit and stared into his face. "I am Gilda, remember me?"

Gilda? he spoke with his eyes.

"Your hospice nurse."

Hospice nurse? he thought. But those are for people who are dying.

She nodded again, as if she heard.

"More morphine," he murmured. His voice worked.

She turned a dial on the pump for the I.V. No relief.

Ziva appeared, worry kneaded into her brow. "Better?" she said. He shook his head. "I've been the worst wife, but I love you so much!" said Ziva, "And so do the kids!" Her pupils were glossy like a reflection in a birdbath. He squeezed her hand. Pain bolted into him again, and he cringed. Ziva pleaded to the nurse, "More morphine!", and Gilda again twisted the dial.

A red light flashed. No more morphine could be given. "More," he whispered, and he watched Gilda put her ear to the pump and thump it. The red light went out. Gilda cranked the dial. The thin tubing that stretched toward him was no thicker than an optical cable. It entered his body as a straw, blasted into the branch of his arm as if from a tornado. The pain diminished to just a scratching at his back. I am dancing, I am dancing, he thought, closing his eyes.

"He's stopped breathing," Ziva said, then realizing more fully, "He's not breathing!"

"Yes," said the nurse, softly, like the last note to a piano solo. With the hum of the machine still pumping, he could feel Ziva's weight slump against his legs near where she had been leaning.

"But he's not breathing," she said again.

True. But he could smell the sweet scent of night blooming jasmine.

# *Divining*

"I feel your liver. It pulsates with the glowing spirit of—" She paused.

"Of *what?*" Ellis asked impatiently. "Does it give any clues to the job market?"

She shook her head, jangling the crescent moons of silver, which dangled from multiple piercings in her ears. She didn't know just yet.

Her fingers hungrily explored the bottom of his foot. She didn't watch her fingers but instead peered at the pastel Buddha on the wall as if he were her brother. All the studio apartment's walls—and even the door of the dishwasher—were painted black. Ellis, surprising himself, groaned as her massaging became more frenzied and more erotic. He lay on the "Table of Spirits," an old couch with its back cut off, while she kneeled at his feet in a ruffled Hungarian peasant's outfit and worked. "You were… saying?" he asked.

She leaned back; only the whites of her eyes showed. She couldn't have been more than twenty years old, almost half his age. Her hands with their delving digits kept pummeling his sole.

She stopped.

"What? What?" he broke in.

Her hands started again, in a slow rhythm as if she were grabbing pencils. "Your left kidney tells me things."

"A palmist at a conference once told me the same thing. What do you hear?"

"I see... I see a car."

"A car? No job?"

"A Chevrolet Monte Carlo, with a blood red interior and an Ankh on the floor."

"But my interior is white."

"Yes?"

"And the Ankh hangs from the mirror. Is— Is what you see my car? What else do you see?"

"I just hear a sound. Like ravens screeching."

"What's that mean?"

She placed his foot between her small breasts, and moved her chest in a counter-clockwise circle. "I can only tell you one thing." She spoke deeply as if she were still connected to his kidney. "You need warmth. I see you need warmth and protection."

"Ravens?"

The young woman sat up straight, straightened her blouse, her hair, then looked at him. "If you want to sleep with me, it's only a little extra."

Ellis stood, caught for words. He left two twenty dollar bills in front of her. "Thanks. I— it's not what I need."

"I think it is," she said, not yet touching the money. "I feel your loneliness."

"We're all lonely. Take the extra twenty and treat yourself to something innocent. Like a hat."


A New Yorker living in West Hollywood, Ellis awoke the next morning twisted in his sheets. Thirty-eight years old and without a job is the way he looked at it. Poverty, he had read somewhere, could age you ten years. That very thought made him take extra doses of choline and zinc for breakfast. As he liquefied celery in his juicerator, he thought he should call his friend Steve, a man who owned a small insurance broker-age.

"Golden Auto Insurance," said Steve in his always cheer-ful talk-radio tone.

"Steve, this is—"

"Ellis!"

"Yes."

"I knew you'd call."

"You did?"

"I learned you might call at the table last night," said Steve. Besides selling insurance, Steve also gave séances. "Al-bert Einstein wandered into the room. My client and he dis-cussed how love was merely a wavelength of light, and then Albert mentioned your name."

"Why would he?"

"He sees everything."

"Steve, I don't know if you also heard, but the computer business is in a slump."

"Albert didn't mention it."

"For the last few months, I've been doing the P.R. for Andrew Gregory, the famous computer guru. He can tell what computer a person should buy just by feeling the per-son's head."

"I could have used him a few months back."

"With the slump, he's writing a book about chocolate. Doubleday's already bought the rights, so he doesn't need me anymore."

"Life is a chariot race, I always say. And the other guy is always Ben Hur."

"Steve, I need a job."

"What?"

"A job. I'm good at selling things. Look at Gregory. Other than his first write-up in *PC World*, he was nothing. Just a schlemiel who tapped on his keyboard. What do you say? Can I work for you?"

"Insurance, Ellis?"

"Sure, insurance!" Ellis had a hard time saying that. He was already breaking out in hives. "People need policies, right?"

"You always say insurance is for losers and lonely wives."

"Double indemnity, I know what that means. I can sell people on that."

"Ellis, calm down. You're such a nervous guy."

"A job, Steve."

"I don't have one... I do have a niece you might like to meet, however—once you get a job, that is."

"I'm looking for a job; you suggest sex."

"Sex!" said Steve surprised. "I'm not saying she's a piece of ass, my God. She's a sweet girl entering a graduate program in library science."

"Steve! Goddamn it, I'm not some lonely hearts club. I'm not looking for a date or a spouse or anything right now."

"Perhaps you should. I sense tension in you, Ellis."

"What? You have Freud with you there?" Ellis slammed down the phone. He kicked the chair for good measure. "I am my creator, I am my creator," he chanted, rubbing his temples. "I am what I create." He kicked the chair again. "Fuck that."


White surrounded Ellis. Nothing was on the walls except for a map of North Dakota. Before him, in a tiny office in downtown Los Angeles, a wiry man right out of "American Gothic" read his résumé. Ellis, in an old-fashioned straight-backed chair, loosened his tie, unbuttoned a few buttons on his vest. A three-piece suit was not what he should have worn. The man wore a stiff corduroy coat over denim.

"Looks goot, looks goot," the man said.

To Ellis's Californian ears, the accent sounded like folksy German. He guessed it was Swedish.

"You look like you're a hard verker. Can I see your hand?"

Andrew Gregory, his last employer, had looked at his hand, also. A strong lifeline and being a Sagittarius got Ellis the job. "I'm a Sagittarius," he said now.

The man paid no attention, and looked at Ellis's calluses instead, feeling their softness. "Your hands vill probably feel tender for, say, the first veek."

"What kind of sales job is this?"

"Yob?"

Ellis's foot bobbed as it always did when he became tense. "Your ad said you got people jobs and you needed people on commission. What is it I'd be selling?"

"The verd is 'commitment,' not 'commission.' I need people med commitment. I tink you misunderstoot."

"Paid by commitment?"

"There's no salary. You pay me."

"For what?"

"For the seminar."

"I pay you!" Ellis's hands threshed the air. "I'm looking for a way to make money, not a way to spend it. Your ad sounded as if it were a job."

"In the lifestyle section?"

"It was?"

"You interested in reaching your potential?"

"Yes, but—"

"You vant to rein your creative energies and never be out of verk again?"

Ellis leaned forward, interested. "Never out of work again?"

"Never again! Four hundred dollars and travel expenses. Grab doze reins and steer ahead to your destiny!"

"Yes, there is a destiny—that's the kind of thing I'm looking for."

"You verk hard, and you grab the brass ring of your potential."

"The I Ching told me to be open to new experiences today. But—"

"Always goot to be open to the new."

Ellis noticed a small stack of brochures on the desk. He picked one up and opened the glossy, four-color pamphlet.

He saw a group of people, various ages, linked in a circle arm-in-arm. "What's the price again?"

"Let me show you our contract."

Ellis signed up and wrote a check. The seminar was entitled "The Ultimate Experience."

"Have you traveled much?" asked the man.

"I've been to Mexico."

"You'll like North Dakota."


Patty Suvan brushed the kinks from her extremely curly hair in the narrow confines of the plane's restroom and with a steady hand glided on some fresh lipstick. She had to laugh as she thought about the hyper man, Ellis Irving, who sat next to her. "Just how is it possible that something as heavy as this multi-ton metal airplane can be held up by air?" he had told her, adding, "Science should not be trusted."

When she had started to explain about airfoils, the little she remembered from the college extension class she took, "How Stuff Works," he smiled as if she had been bamboozled. "My dear," he said. "You are such a trusting soul, I find you refreshing." They had a great conversation about how some things should simply be considered magical, like popcorn, microwave ovens, and Woody Allen movies, when they discovered they were both going for "The Ultimate Experience." She felt more at ease now, getting to know someone who would be there.

As Patty arrived at her row, she smiled to herself. He was a good-looking man. From his tight Lacoste shirt, she could see he worked out a lot—kept himself fit—and the way he smiled and stood up for her was gentlemanly. Even the bald circle on top of his head made him distinguished.

"So why are you doing this Ultimate thing?" he asked as she sat in the middle seat.

"I'm curious. Something 'ultimate' got me intrigued. Of course, my parents think there's something odd about it, but they're great people, really have urged me to always try new things."

"I've never known anyone to have nice parents," he said.

"You haven't? My gosh," she said. "You can borrow mine sometime if you want."

He looked at her surprised, and then seriously, as if she'd said something miraculous. She took it as a compliment.

Ellis didn't say much after that because the plane hit turbulent air and he became sick. "It'll be okay," Patty told him, but his smile and nod couldn't hide the fact he didn't believe her.

The old 737 miraculously did not break apart but landed safely on the Minot runway. As Ellis deplaned, he rocked side to side as if still flying. The only reason he was alive was probably because of the Aztec good-luck figurine he carried with him.

"So this is—" Ellis was going to say "North Dakota" but a curtain of humid furnace air fell upon him. He stopped.

Patty, who was walking behind him, took hold of Ellis's elbow. She had appeared angel-like when she had returned from the restroom earlier. He liked her gentle face and her frizzy dark hair, even if her hair was so thick it kept swishing him in the face. He figured she was in her late twenties—a good age, still full of hope. She now smiled and said, "We're here." He imagined her in a bikini simply because the tan on her shoulders showed two white lines from a bathing suit top. She was probably pretty in a suit.

"North Dakota," she said.

"I gathered."

"Hot, huh? Hot like Huntington Beach. Hope this experience comes with some air conditioning."

Ellis wiped his brow with a handkerchief. "I couldn't agree with you more."

"You okay? You kind of remind me of my grandfather just before his stroke."

"I am not that old!" Ellis pocketed his handkerchief and strode down the stairs without her.

"Sa Ultimate Experience," a begrinned and bearded man shouted in the baggage claim area. He wore a leather vest and jeans and stood tall as a bear. Those who hadn't heard of the seminar—which was most of the plane—moved away.

Ellis, Patty, two young women sporting "Happiness" T-shirts, and a man Ellis's age with a guitar and large belly approached the man. "Are you our ride to the seminar?" Ellis asked.

The man immediately shook Ellis's hand and slapped him on the back. "Velcome, velcome, sa Ultimate Experience, get your bags and step into sa bus out front." He pointed to the glass doors, beyond which stood a green school bus. The words "Towner Baptist Church," its previous owner, appeared ghost-like beneath the paint. The other people scuttled toward the carousel for their luggage, but Ellis stayed.

"You driving?" he asked the man.

"Hans Folkvardt," said the man, and he shook Ellis's hand again.

"Ellis Irving. I was wondering if we could stop at a store on the way. With this heat here, I thought I should get some sea salt tablets, maybe even a little kelp."

"Vhat kind of help? Don't vorry, soon you help yourself."

"Kelp—seaweed. It helps retain body fluids."

"Oh, I see." He grinned as if there were a punchline. "I tink you vill find this a very different place, Mr. Irving. No seaveed here."

"That's okay, that's okay," Ellis said, marking it off as part of the experience.

The ride was bumpy, and Ellis was sure it was damaging his spleen. When Patty, in the seat in front of him, turned around to point out the grain silo coming up, her hair hit him again.

"I've never been east of Las Vegas," she said. "It's kind of flat here. With a few oil refineries, it'd look like El Segundo. No smog, though. That's a good point."

"You sound like a babe out of the woods."

"A babe? Is that a compliment? I think you're making fun of me," she said with a glare.

"No, it's an expression. Please. Sorry." He was surprised at her touchiness. Women. They could be that way.

"What'll you bet the seminar center turns out to be at a farm?" she said.

"A farm?"

"What else is around here?"

He stared out the window at the acres and acres of open land. From the airplane it had looked like a blanket of green dominoes. Here, as they traveled at sixty miles per hour, the combed land vibrated. It was as if the same rows of hand-high plants were in a video loop. Every now and then a white, sharp-roofed box house would break up the scenery. Next to the box would be a missile-shaped silo and a barn. What kind of ultimate experience was this place? Had he been scammed?

"It's supposed to be different," said Ellis, more to himself than to Patty.

They slowed down and took a right turn onto a dirt road. Ellis noticed that the plowed rows on this farm weren't as straight as on other farms. They soon pulled up to a farmhouse nestled in the half-shade of several oak trees. A large woman in a plain blue dress bounded out of the house carrying what looked to be a frosted pitcher of water. Hans, in the driver's seat, greeted her.

"Go' aften!"

"Go' aften. Er det mange arbejdere?"

"Nej—bare fem."

"Fem—det er dejligt."

Hans turned to the members of the bus. "All right, students, off sa bus. My vife, Kirsten, has lemonade, after vhich I vill show you to your rooms."

"Do you think there's sugar in the lemonade?" Ellis asked Patty.

"You a diabetic?"

"No. I guess I could use the electrolytes."

"Here come my brother," said Hans, pointing to a group of people marching off the field. In the lead was a man slightly older than Hans, dressed the same way. He walked backwards as he spoke to the fifteen or so men and women, most of whom were dressed in T-shirts and gym shorts, swim suits or Spandex. They all appeared dirty and sweaty, but most of them looked content.

"Tomorrow ve do something new, fun, and much fulfilling. The vheat become torsty so ve hose tomorrow. Ya?" said Hans's brother to the group.

"Ya," said most of them.

"What are they doing?" asked Ellis to Hans, a bit worried.

"Actualizing," said Hans. "My brother Ole is quite a goot facilitator."

"I'm not sure if I was prepared for this kind of thing," said Ellis.

"No vorry. Ve have two days of classes vhere you learn to open yourself for fulfillment. Dair is exercises for imagery, mind set, and toweling."

"But will this help me get a job?"

"If not in California, den always here."

At the end of one week, after he had hauled himself up daily at sunrise, Ellis slouched in his bed. His body was rebelling. Too much: getting up at 5:30, eating breakfasts of cholesterol and nitrates, sloshing it down with caffeine; having to bathe with a soap whose ph factor was obviously too low; lunches of hog jowls, pig lips, MSG and whatever else they put in hot dogs and hamburgers; sucrose or saccharin for liquid refreshment; dinners of ground steroids on something called cheese bread or pumpernickel, wedges of starch fried in saturated fats, canned vegetables soaked in deadly brine; carbohydrates, protein, and fruits all in the same meal; brownies, cookies, pudding—too much for the system to handle.

He was low.

There was no soya soup or lecithin ice cream. No bee pollen, though he saw plenty of bees. No wheat grass juice, though there was plenty of wheat. And no tofu. He had really done himself in this time.

He expressed his feelings to Hans and was told he was "carrying the wrong baggage" and was unwilling to throw it out.

"Where do I throw it to?" said Ellis.

"For extreme cases, this kind of reaction is normal," assured Hans. "Verk hard and feel fulfillment."

"My stomach constantly rumbles, I have gas, and I'm sure my number five and six vertebrae are out of alignment."

"Relax, watch some TV."

"Mind warp and radiation!"

"Smoke a pipe—I find it relaxing."

"Carcinoma!"

"Have a can of beer and sit on the porch."

"Nitrosamines and aluminum alkaloids!"

"My friend, you've been Californicated. Take the full course and you vill see such a transformation, by golly."

"And the rules. No vitamins, no sex. It's unnatural. Especially with Patty working topless for an overall tan."

"Part of disciplining yourself—you can do it."

He held out his raw callused hand with dirt under the nails, dirt which he couldn't get out. "See the break in my lifeline? I think this farm is the break in my lifeline."

"That's yust vhere your palm folds funny," said Hans.

"I'm dying here."

"Change sometimes feels like death—but then you're reborn."

"There's no magic here," he said, too distraught to do anything about it.

"Then your eyes cannot yet see," said Hans.

Ellis tramped to the fields, day after humid day. He hoed, weeded, and watered, and the wheat began to grow as Ellis continued to droop.

He became more depressed as he acclimated to the hours, the food and the work. He gained five pounds—his arms and legs were stronger than they ever had been—and he became even more despondent. The seminars were few. "How to Focus Your Inner Being on Apple Preserving" and "Your Inner Child and the Art of Weeding" he attended the first week and found them a farce. How could anyone "learn by doing," as Hans had called their work in the fields? True learning meant listening to someone talk.

"You're just a grinch," said Patty as they turned over the farm's compost pile with pitchforks. Patty had volunteered herself and Ellis for the duty, and he went along with it because it saved him from weeding, and he believed in compost. He just didn't know it'd stink so much or there would be so many flies.

"What are you?" said Ellis in reply. "Laura fucking Ingalls Wilder?"

"You didn't even know who she was until I explained her."

"I feel so enlightened."

"You know what's the matter with you, Ellis?"

"Oh, great. I've had this conversation about a thousand times. Last time with my sister."

"Then why don't you listen?"

"I'm a good listener, as any seminar facilitator will tell you."

Patty laughed. "You know, you're a funny guy most of the time, and I mean funny in a good sense."

"As opposed to, say, someone who tells jokes about a girl from Spokane who went to bed with a one-legged man?"

She smirked. Ellis swatted a deer fly on top of his head. Why deer flies liked to bite him hard on his bald spot, he didn't know. He caught the fly in his fingers and he squeezed. Damn fly. It deserved death. It popped with a snap.

"If you'd wear a hat like others, you wouldn't be getting bit there," said Patty.

"They're not hats, they're caps, and I don't want to look like every other hick moron who ever played baseball or drove a John Deere."

"See," she said, adjusting her own baseball cap. "You've just cut down most of the country, including me."

"I don't see you like most of the country."

"I didn't know you even saw me." She threw an extra large chunk of the compost.

"Why would you say that?"

"Ellis," she said with some force like his mother might on a bad day. "You're different than others, which is appealing. You're handsome, you're smart. Why do you have to be so negative sometimes?"

"Because," he said thinking, forking into a section of coffee grounds and brown lettuce leaves. "Because in this life, I'm a rat on a treadmill, running hard to nowhere, and I look to the sides and see other rats, fat and furry, eating cheese and laughing at me."

"Have you figured out yet that maybe all this exercise gives you strength—not only in muscles but also in self-image? You'll be able to take advantage of any new situation."

Her smile looked as if she spent her days at a volleyball court. Christ, how could anyone be so cheerful most of the time? "Leave it to you to find the bright side," he said. "Haven't you ever gotten crushed by a lover? Didn't someone ever die on you? Probably not there in Southern California. If you grew up with Disneyland, horses don't shit. Everyone smiles on Main Street."

Patty glared at him, anger on her face. He had never seen this with her. My god. She threw her pitchfork down, and it speared the earth just before his feet. She turned and walked off, saying nothing.

"Is it something I said?" Ellis asked. She did not reply.

At the end of two weeks, Sunday morning, their only day off, Ellis skipped breakfast and lay in bed, completely naked except for a sheet. He stared at the cobwebs on the ceiling, thinking of what kinds of bugs with what diseases created the black dots that he could discern even his myopic eyes. And why couldn't he have fun lately, when others seemed to enjoy themselves? Was he perhaps spiritualizing his hysteria, as a girlfriend long ago had accused?

He could hear laughter outside his window. People were loading the bus for church. The first Sunday only a few people went, but today it sounded like many more. Ellis thought he could hear Patty's voice among the chatter.

Ellis pulled himself out of bed, not really knowing why it mattered. He pulled back the curtain and could see, indeed, Patty in her long calico dress that she sewed over a few evenings during the week in what was called a sewing bee. Over her form, it looked pleasant. It was the first thing she had ever sewn, she had told him, no longer angry but not explaining why. "Just think about all the people in Los Angeles who might like to sew," she said. "We could start a store, offer classes."

It took for him until now to think about the "we" part. Why had she included him so naturally? He had put her off by laughing and saying he'd rather sell Amway.

As he gazed at her now, ready to climb on the green bus, he sensed that her naiveté was what made her special. She was a kid in a twenty-nine-year-old's clothes. She didn't find this place a horror because horror wasn't programmed into her as it had been with him.

Ellis crawled back into bed and, for the first time ever, wondered why he had ended up doing what he did in Los Angeles, always seeking alternative answers, always promoting other people in his public relations business. Perhaps he should have gone to a shrink instead of so many acupuncturists. He always felt, though, that if he were analyzed, he'd become Woody Allen, unhappy and dependent on some Freudian. Happiness, he thought with a smirk, is as attainable as placenta from a butterfly.

That morning, after he finally dragged himself out of bed after eleven when the church bus still wasn't back, he went to the bathroom down the hall for a shower. He turned the knobs marked hot and cold. Nothing happened. Towel around his waist, he screamed to the kitchen. "Where's the water!"

"No vater!" was the reply. "The vell has gone dry!"

That was the final straw. Ellis wasn't going to spend the day unshowered.

Ellis pulled on yesterday's clothes and searched for Hans. He found him behind the barn in an unplowed field. Hans held the handles of a wishbone-like stick and walked like a beachcomber.

"I'm leaving, Hans!"

"Go ahead, leave." Hans continued on, more concerned with the stick than Ellis's outrage.

"Not until I get a refund, a ride to the airport, and a plane ticket back."

Hans smirked, as if expecting this. "Anyting else?"

"An apology!"

"Ve haff vork to do. Vhy don't you get ready for the day."

"I'm serious."

"So am I."

"I know lawyers! And this place is phony. Your brochure promised spirituality here, a union with life."

"You felt nothing?"

"I felt that not only do you have an inexpensive way to get your farming done, you have people pay you for the privilege of killing themselves in the hot sun. Why buy a tractor when you can have some honest, trusting souls to do the work?"

"Yes, vhy?"

"Because when you break people's trust, they hurt." Ellis aimed at and kicked a clod of dirt toward Hans. It zinged just past Hans's leg.

Hans didn't flinch. Instead, Hans remained concerned with the stick, feeling the ends of the "Y" with his fingers like a surgeon feeling for a nodule.

"And the hurt festers," continued Ellis, "knowing I've been made a fool." Ellis stepped closer. "Look at me!"

Taller and more broad-shouldered, Hans could win in a scuffle, but that seemed the furthest thing from his mind. "I don't tink that our farming gets done med your help vas any secret. No one ever said there vere instant answers here, or that there vere any answers at all. But ve have much to offer here. I am sorry you are blind."

"As if you have anything to see!"

They stood like duelists. Hans's arm came up slowly. "Hold this stick."

"What's it for?"

"Lookin' for vater."

"With a stick?"

Hans nodded. "Got to dig a new vell."

"I don't understand."

"No more vater pressure. *The Farmer's Almanac* told me this vould happen, so this is no surprise."

"You mean to tell me there's some sort of farmers' book of revelations, and you can find water with a stick?"

"Everyone knows these tings."

Ellis stepped closer, took the stick. "What other strange customs do you have?"

"Strange?"

"I mean do, say, bird droppings or something predict the future, anything like that?"

"Ve have crickets. If you listen to their singin' you can tell the veather for the next few days."

"Crickets. I listen to them at night."

"Should I show you how to hold the stick?"

"There's a pattern to the crickets' speech, you say?"

After she returned from the Lutheran services at noon, in such a gloom that she drifted from the minister's questions on what kind of good people could do in this matchhead-quick life, Patty hoped to see Ellis, but he didn't seem to be around. Maybe he had hitchhiked off as he'd been threatening to do. He didn't trust anyone's driving, though, and he always managed to find sticky things on seats, so would he really hitchhike? Unlikely. But maybe she would. She would give Ellis one more chance.

Patty was to meet Ellis at seven o'clock that night at the bus. A small group was going into town for a movie at the Cornfield Six Cineplex. She had convinced Ellis the day before to come when he had said he wouldn't go to church. If she could get his mind off the diseases he knew were rampant, he'd be fine, even if he mentioned that the countryside hadn't done Van Gogh any good. She had liked him from the start for his humor and intensity, but now he seemed to be imploding. He just needed to lighten up.

Ellis was now late. Damn him for treating her this way!

The more she considered his spiral inward, the more she thought about how Hans told her offhandedly in the field one day that people do the darnedest things because they didn't talk. Patty set out to find Ellis. They would talk.

He wasn't in his room, nor at the jellies-and-jams seminar, nor with the group on the upstairs porch waiting for the sunset, still more than two hours away. She even tried the pump house where a group occasionally met to play cards and swap surfing stories. He hated groups, but it was worth a try.

Hans was hosing down the cement landing to the back door. Everyone used the back entrance, and it tended to cake with mud. Boots lined the wall just inside, in two rows straight as pews. "Excuse me, Hans. You see Ellis?" she asked.

"I see a lot in Ellis," he said. "He has much potential."

"No, I mean, have you seen him recently?"

"Ya, sure. Vhat's wrong?"

"Nothing. Just looking for him." Hans looked at her as if to find more meaning. "He's pissed me off. I should have never started talking to him," she said.

"He's interesting, no?"

"No." She sighed, knowing that wasn't true. "He can be funny like my dad," she said. "He reminds me a lot of my dad, I suppose. May he rest in peace."

"I lost my papa, too," said Hans. "Ve all haff so much to do before our final rest."

"I mean, Ellis isn't my dad or anything. Their complaints are so odd—it's really a kind of sensitivity, don't you think?"

"Ya, sure."

"And Ellis is cute, too—but I'm not going to take his disrespect!" She paused. "Ellis thinks I'm too happy."

"Is there such a ting as too much happiness?" Hans bent down to turn the water faucet off.

"No. But who would even think about such things except Ellis? Is it stupid to like someone like Ellis?"

"You two may be like pickle relish, I tink."

"What?"

"You know, med the herring? Pickle relish is the sour and the sweet mixed together—a balance to make the herring go down."

"Maybe so, but I'm not waiting for him anymore," she said with a frown as quick as a gust from the cooling fields. "In fact, I'm probably just going to go back to L.A. soon."

"Ya. Boy, we had a day digging, six of us."

"Pardon?"

"Didn't you hear? Ellis found us vater today, a regular spring. Still, ve had a lot of pipe to lay to connect it to the pump. He really pushed the men. He'd make a good manager."

"He was with that group?"

"Ya."

"So where is he?"

"You hear the crickets tonight?" said Hans. "Sounds like rain."

"I've looked nearly everywhere for Ellis."

He pointed toward the barn. "Try there."


Ellis held the divining rod lightly and continued in his row pattern, still optimistic. Finding the first well had seemed so easy—Hans called it beginner's luck. Now with Hans gone, Ellis was not sensing a thing. Still, he knew if he were logical with his grid pattern and persistent, something would come.

A blackbird cawed—at least it looked black as Ellis watched it float into a thick tree at the edge of the field. Blackbirds, according to Hans, spoke about love. What do farmers need of love when they have 400 acres and more? And what does a caw mean?

With the next caw, Ellis recalled the psychic foot masseuse, the young woman he had visited before this trip. She had heard ravens screeching. Maybe they were blackbirds. These birds. He had needed warmth and protection, she said. She was actually right.

At the end of the row, when he turned, Ellis saw Patty jogging around the corner near the sweet potato patch. "There you are!" she said with a shout.

"Patty, try this! You can feel it vibrate, simply wonderful!

"What're you doing?"

He let the dowser's stick dangle in front of him. "It's called divining. Best I can tell, it takes your unconscious powers of perception and focuses them into the stick. I'm trying to find a second spot for a well."

"Stop goofing around," she told him. "You said you'd meet me at the bus tonight, and you didn't."

He stared at her with a guilty realization. Best to change the subject. "Patty. Who cares about some celluloid fantasies when the powers of the universe are right here?"

"You don't give a shit, do you?" she said.

"What do you mean?"

"Fuck you. You say words, but you don't really talk." She started to walk away.

"Come on. Not this again. Patty? You even swore."

She marched.

"Patty. Come on, this is fun!" he said, but she didn't turn around. "Please."

She turned at that. "You are so incredibly selfish that you may as well just be a hermit crab."

"Oh, that's helpful," he said but decided he should instead keep his response light. "Am I selfish or *shell*fish?"

"Ha ha. See you around."

"Patty! This stick is an interesting thing."

"Don't you think it's hard to compete with a stick?"

"Compete?" he said.

"Ellis, I don't even know why I let you make me angry. You just do."

"Compete? I mean..." He looked hopeful. He noticed the divining rod pointed right at her. "You? Really?"

"Figures."

"What?"

"Nothing, Ellis. I'll tell you about the movie if we happen to run into each other in L.A."

She started tramping away again. Ellis felt as if the sky were moving too fast. If she were competing for him, that meant Patty liked him. He had always liked her, and it had been obvious, hadn't it? Maybe not. Maybe he had to tell her outright—but she was moving away. He dropped the stick.

"Patty! I'm sorry about the bus tonight. And everything. I apologize. Really."

She kept walking. Maybe she didn't hear. Ellis looked around as if someone might help him. Someone or something. Something ultimate. He was drowning there in the field. What could he do to show her? His desperation felt so intense, so horrible, he shouted, "Noooo!"

She turned. He leapt in the air before he knew what he was doing. His body, like the most precise weather satellite, was tracking further reaction. It was her pause that told him he had hope. He pushed himself toward her. He ran knowing the best water was ahead.

# The Rotary

## A

I sit in my grandfather's hospital room. Minutes are like locusts, chewing through my field of time. My grandfather may be dying. I have arrived during visiting hours, nearly missing them thanks to a traffic snarl in the rotary at the Sagamore Bridge. The nurse, who told me to wait in the corner of my grandfather's room, has barely looked at him as she prepares a new I.V. His eyes are closed, and when anyone talks to him, he doesn't respond. I need him to stay alive. He may be able to help me one more time. I stare at my grandfather's prostrate form, and my imagination works overtime.

It is 1918. My grandfather rubs his hands through his thick black hair, not realizing that in a few months he'll be a part of the growing influenza epidemic that will kill 70 million people worldwide. He will live, but the virus will oddly cause him to lose all his hair. He walks with his full head of hair down the streets of Boston, 1918, just after America has entered World War I, thinking he will join the war. He's eighteen and he's fit. He wants to be a lawyer, but the Central Powers must be stopped. He wants to help. He must help. He wonders if he can convince his father of this.

He tells himself he will.

He walks past the Boston Common, a large park, years before there is a parking lot under it for what will be a plague: automobiles. It's only six in the evening, and the sun is making its descent. He steps up a street named Walnut, which is on Beacon Hill, and a street vendor sells flowers. "Flowers, sir?" says the man, who is over twice my grandfather's age.

"Flowers are for funerals," my grandfather replies, but then he remembers where he is headed. He buys four yellow roses—red seems too serious, and twelve would be too extravagant.

He knocks on the door of a young woman named Dorrit, who lives in a building next to one that his future grandson, Jake, my young cousin, will own in another 72 years. Jake will be an investment banker, aggressive in business in a way our grandfather never attains.

Dorrit's father answers the door. He assesses the flowers, nods as if tabulating their cost—both financial and emotional—and invites my grandfather in. They talk about the war in a small room, the library. They speak mostly about the growing American Expeditionary Force and about a battle near Soissons, France. My grandfather gets so involved in the discussion, in fact, that when Dorrit enters, neither he nor Dorrit's father notices her right away.

"I hear the American Military Hospital in Paris is providing fabulous service," says Dorrit's father.

"I'd like to be an ambulance driver there," says my grandfather.

"Bravo, Boy!"

"The American Military Hospital has a number of Fords."

"An excellent auto," says Dorrit's father.

Dorrit clears her throat, and when both men see her, they smile, and my grandfather comments on her fine white dress. A nudge from her father reminds my grandfather of the roses he brought, which he hands her without explanation.

"These are just smashing!" says Dorrit with enthusiasm, who then excuses herself to put the flowers in a vase. That gives my grandfather a chance to finish the discussion. He vows to join the war and drive an ambulance.

Dorrit and my grandfather leave the house and stroll across the widest part of the Common. She holds his arm above the elbow and, at one point, smiles at him, but he does not notice because he is too concerned about his speed. He does not want to walk too fast and make her stumble. They cross Boylston Street and edge their way a few blocks to the Jacob Wirth Company, a restaurant on Sullivan Street. I am named Sullivan, too, but, since I was not yet born, he did not recognize this as a little irony then. His life was full of ironies that he would never get to understand. Another was that he would look more handsome without hair than with.

At this moment in 1918, he only knows he wants to get into Dorrit's knickers, but he does not know how to suggest that and, besides, that's not a good thing for a gentleman to seek in those days, and certainly not one to express. Talk shows and Oprah and the open airing of one's desires have yet to be invented.

"Are you excited about Yale?" Dorrit asks once they are seated at a table and glancing at the menus given to them by a black-vested waiter.

"I might not go right away," says my grandfather. "There's the war."

"Don't be silly. Your studies are more important than a war."

"Why shouldn't I help the allies?"

"You have responsibilities—to yourself, if not your family."

"I might make a good driver."

"Right. Have you tried the rotaries in Boston?" she laughs, referring to the peculiar, often-confusing traffic circles that Boston has been installing for the last few years. But my grandfather frowns. "I'm sorry," she says quickly. "I've never seen you drive."

He says nothing, thinking she resents the fact he does not own an auto. The fact is, she likes him.

"I prefer walking," says Dorrit. "If I didn't have to wear this stuffy dress, I'd even run."

"Run?"

"Why not?"

"That's not very lady-like."

"Why shouldn't girls run?"

He could only respond with a nervous smile and a shrug. This was taking him into territory he had never contemplated. Why would a girl want to run?

"Did I tell you I'll be going to college, too? Bryn Mawr."

"Young women can use finishing."

"Finishing for what?"

"Pardon?" he asks. Why is she questioning his every comment?

"I mean, I don't see it as a finishing school. I want a degree."

"For what?"

"The same as you, maybe. You never know."

He laughs, which seems to jab into her. "I'm sorry," he says. "It's just that you tell me I shouldn't be a driver in the war, that I have to do what's expected, and in the next breath, you say you want to run and to get a degree. Is that what's expected of you?" He thinks he has her. He thinks he's finally put her in her place. But she nods, impressed, much like a fellow would.

She says, "Nothing's really expected of women, don't you agree? Other than we're decorations?"

"It's more complicated than that."

"Not really," she says.

They are silent. Her silence, however, brings his mind back to the war in Europe and being an ambulance driver in Paris. He needs to speak to his father for his blessing. His father thinks America was stupid to get involved in the war but..." Dorrit has just said something.

"Pardon?" says my grandfather.

"I do think the daffodils are pretty in that vase," she says, pointing to the dark mahogany bar. He sees the stupid flowers.

He wonders what the hell is wrong with the roses he bought her? Roses make a damn nice flower, and now she wants daffodils?

He does not notice the motto over the bar, "Suum Cuique," which his Latin studies at Milton Academy should have allowed him to translate, "To Each His Own"—but he is too upset to be aware of such things at that moment. They eat quickly when their food arrives. They talk very little. He takes her home directly. He plans to never date her ever again. At the door, she turns and is about to say something and stops. Looking into his eyes, she becomes transfixed.

"What?" he says.

"Nothing. I— I just never noticed you had green in your blue eyes." She keeps looking.

"Doesn't matter. I can still see."

"They say green eyes are a sign of genius."

He pauses. She's smiling—and waiting. His heart is beating fast, like it never has before, and he knows this girl is better than any radio transmission he has ever heard, and her lips—she's offering her lips, lips that Michelangelo could have carved. He kisses her—nothing marble about her—and he cannot think the same way anymore.

He forgets about becoming an ambulance driver.

He attends Yale in the fall and takes more Latin.

He proposes to Dorrit at Christmas and she accepts.

That's the problem with our family: we seem to be impulsive when it comes to love. Still, it worked for him. Was it the long engagement? What's the secret?

# B

M y bald-headed grandfather remains asleep in his hospital bed—or is he comatose? I am utterly confused and at a loss. I am 28, running a very small and quaint hotel on the Cape. My grandfather has had a stroke, which has brought him to the hospital, and I have been sitting, my mind wandering to the possible past. Watching him makes me wonder if it's better to know you are dying, and you can experience death and whatever wonders it has, or is it better to be asleep? After a stroke, can you make sense of reality anyway?

The mind does funny things. Mine now flits to my parents, who met right near here, near the Cambridge Hospital.

My mother at age 22 stands in a long skirt and a pretty pink blouse by a particular entrance to Harvard University waiting for Henry, her new beau who, unknown to her, is off buying a ring. They have had three dates, and already he wants to marry her. This is 1951, and she is a Radcliffe graduate student, the third of five children, and she does not know Henry's intentions. In fact, though she likes him, she's wondering if this is the time to have a beau. Maybe she should stop seeing him. She has school, after all, and all the Harvard boys think Radcliffe girls are just looking for a husband, but she's not. She wants to be taken seriously and eventually run her own company.

She looks at her watch with irritation. Where the hell is Henry? She wants to get to the Brattle Theatre before the matinee of Moliere's *Imaginary Invalid* starts. Is Henry not taking her seriously? She will give him five more minutes, and then she will go to the theatre without him. After all, the play stars Zero Mostel. Blacklisted in Hollywood, Mostel has yet to testify before the House Un-American Activities Committee, not naming names. He has spoken out against Senator Joseph McCarthy and against those in Hollywood who follow in McCarthy's witch-hunting footsteps. My mother thinks Mostel is brave. His next film and television work will be a long time in coming, at the end of the decade. Even without the evidence of how many careers McCarthy will ruin, she thinks McCarthy is a criminal.

Henry does not know she feels this way because they have not talked politics. They are opposite in many ways, but they don't know that. They have had only three dates.

My mother notes the misspelled words chiseled into stone at the entrance: "...that the colledge agreed upon formerly to bee built at Cambridg shalbee called Harvard Colledge." Christ, she thinks. Can't they fix the spelling now that people know how to spell? This is Harvard, after all.

Henry, a graduate student in the Harvard Business School, comes running up in his scratchy wool suit, fedora hat, and Cutty Sark smile. If he were in Hollywood and an actor, women by the thousands might swoon. He is handsome. My mother's heart patters a little more. "Whew!" he says. "Sorry—the subway was running late."

"Thought I'd have to leave without you," says my mother.

"You wouldn't have done that, would you?" says Henry. A look flashes across his face as if he's been insulted.

"They would have held your ticket at the box office," she says. My mother, who from pure habit knows how to make boys feel good, adds, "I would have missed you." She touches her brown, shoulder-length hair.

His smile returns. "I was wondering if we might go to the Hotel Cambridge after the play," he says.

My mother looks at him anew. Although this is a new age and she smokes cigarettes and has her own Studebaker President, a convertible, she feels he's presumptuous. She's not that kind of girl.

"The hotel for dinner," he quickly adds, seeming to interpret her expression. "It's a nice place."

"The hotel restaurant would be pleasant," my mother says, adding a smile that has turned many a head before him. "I like that place. Thank you."

They enjoy the matinee, laugh at Mostel as a rich man, Argan, who imagines things are constantly wrong with his health and who tries to wed his daughter to a doctor. A son-in-law doctor would give him constant medical attention. His daughter, however, loves another man—poorer, of course, and not a doctor. The play is all about marrying the right person. In the audience, Henry and my mother hold hands. Meanwhile, Argan's second wife, while seemingly doting on the old man, schemes for his fortune. No one sees the way things are.

Afterwards, Henry wants to go straight to the restaurant, but my mother wants to stop at her apartment on Harvard Street to change clothes.

"You look fine," he says. They walk in circles.

"Not for a place as nice as the Hotel Cambridge. You're always rushing me."

"I'm never an 'always'."

"Sure you are. You're always sweet to me."

Her smile comes again, and he nods. She takes his hand as they walk toward her place. He looks at his watch, however, as if to emphasize that time is an element. He's as bold as her father, my grandfather, but Henry is, for her, much easier to talk to.

They cross Boylston Street—the same street my grandfather had crossed years earlier with his lady friend, but in a different part of town. My mother and Henry are not far from Harvard's Stillman Infirmary, where students had been treated and died after the terrible influenza epidemic had reached Cambridge in the last month of the First World War. Henry is unusually quiet.

"Did I say something wrong?" my mother says, noticing.

"No. Why?"

"You seem so contemplative."

"I'm just thinking."

"What're you thinking?"

"Eisenhower," he says, seeming to obscure what he was thinking. "He'd make a good president."

"You're nuts," says my mother. "Adlai Stevenson is the better man."

"He's too stiff."

"He's smart. You think Ike is smarter?"

"You're a Democrat?"

"I don't know. Maybe."

"Ike will get the nomination—Taft is too conservative—and he'll get us out of Korea." Henry appears uneasy.

She realizes she's supposed to agree with what he says. They're on a date, after all. Still, she can't help herself. "Eisenhower is a general, and generals like wars," she says.

"You're wrong there. Generals want to stop wars."

"What do you know?" says my mother as she gathers her keys, irritated.

"Nothing," he says as he looks away, angry.

My mother is not good at agreeing with everything a man says, true, but when she sees his face, gnarled on one side like the wrinkles on a drying apple, she realizes she'd better switch topics quickly. "If you want me to go to the restaurant in this, I can do so," she says. "Maybe you're right: we should go directly."

"Why? You in a hurry for the date to be over?"

"Don't be silly. I'm having a marvelous time."

"We're almost to your place, so you may as well change."

At the apartment, my mother's roommate, Barbara, is not in. Barbara earlier in the week had become engaged and will marry soon, which means my mother will have to find another roommate for the spring term. This is on her mind. My father, apparently seeing my mother look worried, pulls her toward him, and they kiss.

The hotel is expensive and elegant. The restaurant is classy. A few years earlier, in fact, a Harvard alumnus, John F. Kennedy, announced his candidacy for the Congress of the United States from its George Washington Ballroom. Kennedy, a product of the times, optimistic and forward looking, will later intone as president, "Ask not what your country can do for you; ask what you can do for your country," an attitude that starts to change when a bullet rips through his skull on November 22, 1963, years after this September night where my mother catches her reflection in a gilded mirror. My mother is glad she has changed. The dress looks good.

Henry suggests oysters, but my mother says she hates oysters, sorry. He gets shrimp cocktail. He asks her if she'd like a Manhattan, but she prefers, she says, a white wine. He asks the waiter for a wine list. He knows nothing about wine.

Forty years later Henry will be an expert on wine and in re-
tirement will have his own vineyard, but this day he just
points at a white one randomly, yet purposefully, as if it's the
white wine he's had a hundred times. One of the great quali-
ties of Henry, she realizes, is that even in doubt he looks assured, an attitude that comforts people. He smiles. The
waiter smiles. My mother smiles. Everyone is happy. When
the waiter leaves, Henry looks ponderous.

"You okay?" she asks.

"Never better than when I'm with you." He beams, but
still it looks like he's masking something. Was he still upset
about her comments on Ike? Maybe she should talk about a
topic they can agree on.

"I like Professor Clark," my mother says, commenting on
their professor. It is Clark's class they met in, the one-and-
only class created as an experiment in coeducation for the
two colleges.

"He's a jerk," my father says.

"Really?"

"He seems to pander to the women. When a woman asks
a question, he waxes on as if he's King Lear adoring his
daughters."

"I think I ask good questions."

"Oh, yes, you do, I didn't mean—"

"You don't mind the fact that females are in business
school?"

"If you're good at something, what's wrong with that?"
He looks earnest. Good, she thinks.

The wine comes. They drink a few glasses with bread and
order food. My mother soon is laughing. This is the first time
she has ever had more than one glass of wine in an evening.
They talk about things they can agree on.

"I love your hair," he says.

She touches it, lets her finger pull it out from behind her
ear. It's sensuous; she smiles. Unknown to them, for the word
and concept won't even be created for eight more years,

pheromones are emanating from both of them, enhancing the attraction. Biology is at work.

Henry draws his hand from his pocket, and he holds something in his closed hand. He opens his hand to reveal a small velvet box. It takes her breath away—this is too quick. He hands it to her, and she opens it with trepidation.

"What's this?" she says, staring at the silver ring sparkling with five small diamonds.

"This is why I was late. I wanted the perfect ring for the perfect girl. What do you think?" And with a flourish, he gets to his knees, causing others nearby to notice. He clasps his hands like a monk and quotes in verse from the play they just saw—Henry has always been a fast thinker. "Your hand, my dear, is wanted in a mating. You laugh? Perhaps you've been anticipating that I want to marry you."

"Marry?" Her face now shows more astonishment than horror. She's thinking of how her roommate will be delighted, how other friends will be envious. She notices that he looks a little worried. Will she accept? People nearby have noticed his proposal—how romantic!—and they clap. She thinks isn't this what she eventually hoped for? Yet a few doubts quickly cross her mind: Will she finish grad school? Will she start her own business? Then again, Henry's father has money, and money isn't bad, and maybe she and Henry might start a business together.

"Well?" he says. "How about it, Sport?"

She thinks how good she'll look in a gown, how her parents will be pleased, how handsome Henry is, how handsome their children will be, how how how how can she say no? But she should say no, this is crazy, this is not the time to fall for a boy. But he looks so hopeful. The people at the next table, a balding man and a gray-haired woman look happy. She and Henry could be happy like them at that age, she thinks. She could be happy like her parents. This must be right.

Should I shout from the sidelines, "No, no, no?" That you will marry and divorce and marry and divorce, like yo-yos searching for the perfect spin? Should I say that Henry, my father, is a wonderful man, but they're not right for each other, and my sister and I will be confused? That we, too, as adults, will join the spin of serial marriages? Then my own biology, too, impulsively calls: marry, marry—make me be. Let me grow up and sail with my grandfather and learn about running with the wind.

"I'd love to," my mother says, and she kisses Henry, and people clap.

# C

I am shaken awake. I see a thin arm at first—my grandfather's?—then look up into the fifty-year-old face of a woman with blond hair. "Mom," I say. "What're you doing here?"

"How long have you been here?" she asks.

I glance at the clock on the wall and see it's after two in the morning. No one has kicked me out. My grandfather sleeps on his back, mouth open, snoring. He looks as he does at home, not like a man in a coma.

"This is a funny time to be visiting," I say.

"I couldn't sleep. I don't know. I had a funny feeling." She's dressed in a white suit and lavender blouse as she might wear to a meeting with advertisers. She owns her own advertising company.

"What do you mean?" I ask.

"That he might not make it much longer," she says. "I needed to see him again."

"Me, too," I say, and we look at each other honestly. Fifty isn't so bad, I think. She and I haven't seen each other a lot since I married. She doesn't like Geneva much. Geneva doesn't like her much. Hence, Mom and I have had short conversations on the phone every few weeks.

She stares at her father. "I'm kind of jealous of you," she says.

"Me? Why?"

"This isn't a man who got very close to his children, yet you two seemed to connect like no one else."

"None of you," I say, referring to her and her siblings, "had the same interests as he—particularly photography and sailing."

"I just didn't understand him—or your father."

"Dad and Grandpa are alike. You hang with them awhile, and they talk. I listen. I like them."

"Maybe I'm not a good listener." She has that right, but I don't say a thing because I realize she and I are alike in another way—we understand people of the same sex but not the other. For some reason, Geneva hates my listening. I don't get why. She says I'm a watcher and accuses me of not saying what I feel. When I'm honest with her, though, it's like squirting lighter fluid onto red-hot coals. She swears and accuses me of being insensitive.

My mother and I watch the last half of a movie on the TV. It's about a Scottish cat trying to get back to its home after it dies. With cats having nine lives, it uses a couple more lives to get back to the little girl who loves her. Patrick McGoohan plays the little girl's insensitive father, and when the father at the end hugs his daughter, I notice tears come to my mother's eyes. She becomes flustered, wiping her eyes as if her body has betrayed her.

"This is silly," she says. "It's just a stupid old film, and we're watching it as he's dying." It's also hard on her as her mother, my grandmother, has Alzheimer's.

Mom gets up, kisses her father on his cheek, and I stand. She hugs me and holds on longer than I remember her ever doing. She kisses me on the cheek, too. "I love you," she says.

"I love you, too."

"I didn't even know how to diaper you at first, and now here you are." She's said this before, as if once you're diapered, you're a man.

After she leaves, I ponder just how it is I got here. There was the diaper when I was born, and then there was the road today. In between, there was a small little rotary five years ago where a woman bashed into my new green Honda Accord hatchback from behind.

I picture it now. I leap out of my car, ready to yell at some jerk who shouldn't have a license, but getting out of the car is a woman with long frizzy hair and red halter top as bright as strawberries. She's like a troll with beautiful skin and a figure. It's not as if I have a moment to appreciate her splendor before she barges toward me, a female Napoleon, and yells, "You asshole! Why the hell are you stopped on a rotary?"

"I wasn't stopped," I explain. "I was going slowly. I wasn't sure which road I had to take, so—"

"Some of us need to get places," she says.

Cars like colored jellybeans are honking at us because we're stopped, but she waves them around. When one person beeps his horn, she gives him the finger.

"Maybe we should get off this rotary," I say. "Or we'll get hit again."

"Where did you get your license—from a Cracker Jacks box?" she says.

What's with this woman? I suggest we take the next right because it looks like there's a parking lot. She agrees.

Once there, we exchange licenses. Mine is not from Cracker Jacks. Hers is from New York, which figures, with her mouth.

"Do you have insurance?" I ask.

"I'm going to B.U. It's all I can do to pay for tuition," she says. She gasps as if only now she's starting to comprehend it's her mistake. I can see tears, but she's wiping them away as she's looking at her front bumper, which is bent. My back bumper is worse.

"The law is that if you hit someone from behind, you're at fault," I say.

"What are you, a lawyer?"

"I'm a night accountant at a large hotel," I say, proud of my first job, not thinking how my job puts me out of sync with most people. I'm night. She's day.

"It's a new car, too, isn't it? Shit. I'm sorry."

"I'll have my insurance company call you." I examine her license carefully and write out her name and address. "What's your phone number?" I ask.

"Why?" she says.

"Aren't you listening?" I ask.

"I thought you're asking me on a date."

I look at her. She's now smiling. The sun is behind her, and her thick long hair glows like she's on fire. The red top isn't bad, either. I don't realize many things in that moment including the power to procreate can bend steel, melt glass, and reshape bumpers and lives. Hydrogen fuses on the surface of the sun, shooting gamma rays into my eyes and onto her unblemished skin. This all happens before I can imagine other things, such as a wedding in the woods of Maine or the way she looks twirling a lock of her hair as she sips coffee and reads the *Boston Globe*.

"I'd love to ask you out," I say, and I hold out my hand. "My name's Sullivan."

"Geneva," she says, and shakes mine.

Our lives turn on the stupidest things.

# D

My grandfather's eyes open, and the two pale blue oases with flecks of green move amid his wrinkly pale desert skin. He focuses on the white, acoustically pocked ceiling above him, then on the muted TV that silently promotes a fire—news at ten. Maybe he thinks he's dead and this is the strange place he's been sent. The afterlife. When he sees me, he looks surprised, then smiles—or at least I think it's a smile. Mona Lisa. He seems to recognize me. That makes me feel as if a whole Italian plaza of doves has just taken flight.

"Hi, Pa," I say.

He points to me with his left pajamaed arm. He gets to wear his favorite green pajamas, which is good to see.

"I arrived late," I say, "but I got stuck in a rotary."

My grandfather says something, or at least his mouth is moving, and I think perhaps he is actually talking, even though the nurse says he can't. I place my ear near his mouth and hear him. He says, "Get a push-button phone."

"You're talking!" I shout, only then realizing he was making a joke about rotary dial phones. "And you're still funny! Do the others know?"

"I don't think Dorrit has ever thought me funny."

"No, I mean do people know you can talk?" I say.

"I've had nothing to say."

I laugh this time. He's referring to a joke he used to tell about a talking dog that, when taken to a bar, doesn't talk, and the owner loses a lot of money on bets. At home, the dog starts to talk again. "Why didn't you say anything at the bar!" the owner yells, and the dog says, "Because I had nothing to say."

"You had nothing to say to the nurse or grandma?" I ask now.

Grandpa just shrugs with his left shoulder, emphasizing how he's paralyzed on his right. "How's Geneva?" he asks in his whisper. I think of quipping something about Switzerland.

"Fine," I say. "She's selling Fords now, did I tell you? Top salesperson for the month." I don't mention that Geneva surprised me earlier this week by saying she was moving out. Since our small house is part of the hotel I run, she couldn't very well ask me to move. She said we weren't "working." Marriages are like oil derricks and motorboats; when they don't work, they're abandoned. How'd Mom-Mom and Grandpa have such a good life? What's the secret?

"What's new?" my grandfather says, which startles me, but I see he's been looking at my face as much as I had looked at his when he slept. "Are you enjoying yourself?"

"Yes," I say. "Sure."

"You don't sound very enthusiastic."

I've often felt incredibly transparent with my grandfather, as if he could read my source code thanks to our hours of sailing.

He was there when I was seven to explain how my father's leaving wasn't because of me. How could I ask him to give me new words now to keep me sane? Besides, I should be there for him, not me.

"I'm just in a rough spot is all—but not as rough as you."

"Dying is not rough. It's inevitable, like crabgrass."

"You're not dying!"

"Sullivan. I know it's coming." He says this with such conviction, even if it's in a whisper, that I sense he may be right.

"Sullivan," he whispers, touching me with his good, left hand. "What's going on with you? Something at home?"

"You're dying! Isn't that enough?"

"What's going on?" he says patiently.

I haven't told anyone, not even my parents. My grandfather, though, looks at me with his kindly eyes. He seems the right first person to tell. I gather my strength.

"We seem to be splitting up. She said I'd become too comfortable. Isn't that our goal?"

"So how do you feel?" he asks.

"What am I supposed to be, some kind of combination gondolier and stand-up comic? I have passion! I can use exclamation points!" I say, trying to be light when, in fact, I'm lightheaded. "It's been hard to stay afloat financially, what with bills and a wife who is up-and-down in her car sales abilities. But I've been working harder than ever." I'm in my father's long-ago shoes, I realize, attempting to create a career and about to leave a marriage behind.

"And you want to stay?"

"Yes! I keep thinking about what's in my past—or your past or my parents' past—that connects me to what's happening now? The world is tumbling down, and I can't say why."

Grandpa sits up in bed, swings the IV line over his shoulder as smoothly as John Travolta on the dance floor, and moves so he's facing me, his feet on the ground. He seems to shake off his paralysis as easily as the blanket.

"Did I ever tell you the fable about the rattlesnake and the dog?"

I shake my head, no, amazed he's talking and acting like he just woke up from a nap. "You have a lot of dog stories," I say.

"I do. A dog is walking along a riverbank one day when he's stopped cold by the sound of a rattlesnake, which is poised, ready to strike and kill him. The dog, frozen for a second, leaps out of the way when he hears the snake say, 'Please, kind dog, don't leave me. I need to get across the river, and maybe I could get on your back and you can take me across.'"

My grandfather says this with a high voice and a smile. He's back in form.

Grandpa continues: "'Why don't you swim?' says the dog. 'Rattlesnakes don't swim,' says the snake. 'If I take you, though,' says the dog, 'You'll bite me and I'll die.' 'No, I won't,' the snake promises, 'because I'd drown, too.' So the dog lets the snake slither on his back, and the dog starts swimming across. Halfway over, the dog hears the snake's rattle and soon feels the snake bite him in the neck. The dog instantly starts to flounder and yells, 'How come you bit me!' And the snake, starting to drown, too, says, 'Because it's my nature.'"

My grandfather hits his knee and laughs hard. "Because it's my nature," he repeats, getting under the covers.

"What's that have to do with my divorce?" I say.

"Maybe nothing," he says.

"What did I do wrong?" I protest.

"Some things just are," he says. "Independent women are independent. Dorrit has always been a handful—and has your mother. Geneva, too—that why we've loved them." He winks.

We are quiet for a minute, which allows me to soak in his strength. I notice how the television is silently showing a soap opera. A handsome jerk in a tuxedo is on his knees begging something from a standing and breast-enhanced woman in a negligee who is wiping tears from her mascaraed eyes. He pulls out a velvet box. She opens it. It's a wedding ring. I shake my head. They mock what is real.

I look at my grandfather. Eighty-three years he's lived on this earth—not even enough to make a decent layer of sandstone, geologically speaking. Even so, he means everything to me. I touch the skin on his hand. It is smooth and cool. The thought of stone makes me think of marble. I don't want him under marble yet.

"What's the secret?" I ask.

"What secret?"

"How to have a happy marriage."

"How do any of us do it?" he says. "We're all slammed with the unexpected."

"Geneva's gone."

"I know. You're still a good person."

Right.

"Just go and love, Sully. You'll make it. You'll do well," says Grandpa.

I can't say anything. Still, these are the right words. The fingers that have strangled my stomach for days loosen.

"Sully, did you hear me?" he says. I think he says. It looks like his paralysis has come back.

I'm crying. I can't help it. I haven't cried since I was probably ten. My whole body shakes. He doesn't move at all. Boys don't cry, but here I'm losing everything, and yet he has helped me once again, and my body can no longer restrain itself. I shake and cry and shake and cry.

I stare at the still form of my grandfather.

A nurse enters, a different one from before, a woman much older than me, gray-haired, kindly. Tray in hand, she's as elegant as someone on a postage stamp. She looks at me, seeing me wiping my tears, then looks over at my grandfather. She hurries in, slams the tray on the table, and desperately tries to hear for his breath. It's not there. He's gone.

This world always tests me when I don't want to be tested. I don't want my own next breath. My body rebels, though, and my mouth breaks open for air like a diver who had been down too far. I imagine my grandfather's hand running through his black hair. I imagine him buying roses, this time a dozen, for his wife to be, my grandmother. He adds some daffodils. That image gets me through the next few minutes. If you can hold on through the worst parts by thinking of something good, I tell myself, then maybe you can make it.

# Shooting Funerals

S triving for success is like riding a crazy kangaroo, Vicky Tomlinson thought. Not that she had ever ridden a kangaroo. Sports entertainment was one of the few professions she had not tried. Elementary school substitute teacher, Hyundai salesperson, and Zamboni driver for preparing an ice rink daily at a high school—she had been all these within the last three years, as well as a photographer's assistant. She was getting tired of so much change, in fact, that all she wanted was a little stability.

"It's hard reaching the end of your thirties," she told her marriage counselor. Not that she and Bruce were married, but they wished to be, or rather Vicky wished to be. Bruce wanted to live like his parents, who had never married after forty-two years.

"I want kids," Vicky said. "And I want them in a marriage. These are signs of a stable life."

"But if you think about the universe—which I do at 37,000 feet," said Bruce, an airline pilot, "the universe doesn't care if people are married or not. When you think about all the space and all the millions and billions of years gone by, we're just a fraction of an eye blink."

"What's that have to do with us?"

"Happiness is more important than a piece of paper, isn't it?"

"Your happiness or Victoria's?" asked Dr. Graybill, a female psychologist as true and homely as an artichoke. "A union of any sort includes compromise."

"I don't see the big deal about being married. We can have kids anytime," Bruce said in what Vicky felt was his homunculus way. He was short and balding and had a sibilant "S" that hissed like an old bicycle tire, but Vicky knew he thought he was a catch. "Besides," Bruce stressed, "can you imagine sticky peanut butter fingers over our sanitary white walls?"

While they continued their twice-monthly sessions, Bruce's uncle died in the Bronx after slipping on the cellophane from a new video his wife had unwrapped and had left on the floor. He had hit his head on the coffee table. The video was *Out of Africa*. "Shame he didn't get to see it," Vicky told Bruce. "Meryl Streep's accent is impeccable."

She and Bruce attended the funeral in Queens. At that point she had been a photography assistant for a full year, and her day rate was up to what some of the best were charging. She could assemble a light box and put it on a C-stand within minutes. She could unload and load a Hassy in under sixty seconds, which is important if the photographer was shooting a wedding or any real life event in film. Digital cameras were not as demanding, but many photographers still liked working in the larger film format. For the first time in years, Vicky felt this was perhaps what she was meant to do. She yearned to be a full-fledged photographer with her own clients.

At the graveyard, she quietly shot with her digital Pentax as Bruce's uncle's pine casket was removed from the hearse by four short, union gravediggers in baseball caps and green uniforms like those worn by garage mechanics. None of Bruce's relatives were pallbearers, Vicky noted. It was the first Jewish funeral Vicky had attended, though she had assisted at many a bar mitzvah, a staple for some New York photographers. The little green men lowered Bruce's relative into the hole.

The widow, Bruce's aunt, dressed in a stylish black dress and veil, modeling much gold jewelry over a tan, did not shed a tear when she threw a handful of dirt onto the wooden box. Next to her, in contrast, a dumpy-looking stout man was pushing against an equally rotund woman, trying to get around her.

"It's my turn," said the man. "I'm oldest."

"He liked me better. I was a better sister to him than you were a brother to him or me," said the woman who, like her brother, was in her late-fifties and wore an oversize beige coat.

To Vicky, they looked like twin burlap sacks of Idaho russets. Brother and sister each picked up a handful of dirt and threw them into the grave at the same time.

Bruce laughed when he came up from behind Vicky at her computer and saw a slideshow of the shots. "Honey, these are great," he said. "You really captured their personalities." He pointed to the pictures of his two cousins, the potato-like brother and sister, glaring at each other. "They work with each other at a post office, and they fight all the time."

Vicky clicked to enlarge a particular thumbnail. The widow, Bruce's aunt, grinned with a cigarette in one hand and a beer in the other. The after-service party had been lively.

"My aunt," said Bruce, "had been having an affair with my uncle's partner, who will now control the restaurant, The Fun Steer. The place is a virtual cash cow." He pointed to a tall thin man in the next photo. "He even has a smirk on his face, doesn't he?"

A toilet flushed in the apartment above them, and footsteps could be heard. Vicky pictured her bearded ex-husband, Jeffrey, a humorless printer who still lived there, washing his hands endlessly like a monk who had just sinned. Vicky had left him for their downstairs neighbor, Bruce, two years earlier.

"We need to move," Vicky said.

"How?" said Bruce. "We've gone over this. I've had this apartment fifteen years with rent control. It's a deal."

"He's probably rubbing her belly right now," she said, pointing to the ceiling. "Like it's some big, fat crystal ball." Since the divorce, her ex-husband had married a woman named Stacy, a receptionist with large breasts. Stacy was presently pregnant. When Vicky saw Stacy lumber out the front entrance recently, Vicky felt envious. Vicky had no time to lose if she wanted a child.

"Christ," said Bruce. "You hear and imagine things no one else can. Reality is that you need to find out what makes you happy," said Bruce.

"Getting married would make me happy."

"Maybe for a week," he said. "But that's external. True happiness is from within."

"I was also thinking of getting into business."

"There you go. I've always said you need to find a job you really like."

"I was thinking of turning this into a business," Vicky said, pointing to her screen.

"Being a photographer?"

"Shooting funerals. Until other photographers catch onto the idea, I'll have the market to myself. After all, funerals bring a lot of relatives together. People will want to remember."

"Vicky. I'm talking about a real job."

"Me, too."

Vicky fell into her first opportunity a month later when her college roommate, Susan from Flushing, New York, lost her 86-year-old grandfather. He was to be buried in Cranbury, New Jersey, not too far away. Susan had asked her grandmother if she had booked a funeral photographer yet. Susan said her grandmother had panicked, as if she'd forgotten. Susan landed Vicky the job.

"Cripes," said Bruce to Vicky that night. "You're not serious about this thing?"

"At least someone believes in me," Vicky replied, referring to Susan.

"Susan's a travel agent," said Bruce. "They always think they're sending you to good places."

"You don't want me to be successful."

"A funeral photographer, Vicky?"

"Look at you. Your flight paths are mapped out by management. You fly to the same cities over and over. And Tuesdays you make meatballs, every Wednesday is fish."

"Not your meatballs-and-fish speech again!"

"Everything is ultra-planned in your life. I'm always here, right? So why marry me?"

"Vicky, Vicky. You just don't see."

"I'm sure someone told Thomas Edison that the electric light bulb was a terrible idea, too."

Vicky prepared for the funeral with a list of shots she knew she must get, much as she might in preparing for any other traditional event. It had to tell the story of the day. "Box of Kleenex," she wrote to remind her to shoot a close-up of someone pulling out a tissue. "Gray partial" she wrote as a memo to herself to buy a filter with a gray top half. It would add an overcast to the sky in case it was a bright, sunny day.

The day started well enough with shots of family and friends gathering outside a New Jersey church. Shouts of glee brought together those who hadn't seen each other in years. "Sorry it took such a sad occasion to see each other" was often the refrain. People accepted Vicky's presence easily, often requesting her to take pictures of them. Susan's oldest brother Michael, however, dressed in a worn suit slightly too small as if he hadn't bought a suit since college, was the exception. He glared at her. "What's his problem?" Vicky wondered.

The service started on time, and Vicky shot the rail thin, white-robed Episcopal priest moving from the church's sacristy into the chapel with six pall bearers and other bereaved family in tow. A teen-aged grandson in the family accidentally stepped on his aunt's long black skirt, pulling it down and revealing a tattoo of a tarantula on her upper thigh. That caused much whispering, as did Vicky's friend Susan, who—dressed in a Knockwurst-colored dress—banged into the rich mahogany casket when Vicky, rushing up, clicking away, startled Susan. The casket fell from its stand with a thud.

A problem occurred at graveside when Vicky tried to set up a shot with her friend Susan throwing in a handful of dirt on the casket. That had been such a moving moment at the Jewish funeral. "What are you doing!" intoned the priest. "I do the ashes-to-ashes part—not anyone else."

"I'm sorry. Would you then mind doing the ashes stuff a little farther to the left?" whispered Vicky. "I can get some nice back-lighting by the sun."

"What's a photographer doing here!" cried Susan's brother, Michael. "This is ridiculous!"

Their grandmother, the widow, looked shocked and blurted, "But Susan said...."

"Susan!" bellowed Michael. "You've ruined the whole day!"

Vicky nonetheless thought she could save the situation by getting them involved. "Could the immediate family could get closer together? You might look somberly into the grave. That'll make a good shot. Right after that, if I could get just the pall bearers doing the same thing, that'd be great."

"Out of here, out of here!" shouted Michael moving toward her. Vicky shot his angry approach, which infuriated Michael more. Susan, trying to stop her brother, leapt onto his back. A cousin tried to pull Susan off. Susan's youngest brother, Nathan, a manic-depressive on a heavy dose of lithium who smiled with glee, appeared sure he could be a hero and ran full speed toward the group, bashing into them. The loose dirt and gravel around the hole added to the situation. The four young people lost their balance and fell into the grave. Gravel and shoes hammered loudly against the coffin lid. Scrambling on top of the coffin, Michael gasped in utter anguish as if he were dancing on radioactivity.

Vicky guessed it was a good time to leave. The priest, shoving her toward the parking lot, was another indicator.

On the way home, Vicky pictured in her mind all the shots she invented but did not get: the executor's cutting of the cake at the reception, the widow's tossing of a faded rose—both of which she thought might become standard shots at funerals. Her best creation would have been having the family stand in two rows, their backs to each other to create a corridor where no faces could be seen. The main bereaved person, in this case the widow, would then solemnly walk down the aisle of backs, throwing rice on everyone's shoulders, symbolizing, Vicky felt, tears as well as the idea of rebirth.

Vicky almost threw up as she drove back into the dark, frenetic city. She felt choked by an invisible shroud, and throwing up might be a relief. Bruce would surely mock her for her failure in her enterprise. He would never marry her, she realized. *We're all like mollusks in dim, cold waters*, she thought. What kind of mollusk? She pictured the word "abalone" and then realized it had the word "alone" in it. That's what she was. Alone. She had been alone since sixteen, after her father had died from a heart attack, and, shortly after, her mother died of cancer. Bruce could never understand the separateness this created. Bruce would be better as a floor wax.

Taxis and cars kept cutting her off on the Henry Hudson Parkway, and a homeless person with a spray bottle at a left turn lane took one look at her scratched and dented yellow Volkswagen Beetle and, rather than try for her business, moved to the windshield of the Mercedes behind her. She felt depressed.

When she found a parking spot on 97th Street near Broadway, she felt momentarily lucky. A good parking spot could wipe out a lot of grief. Then she saw her ex-husband Jeffrey assist the pregnant Stacy into their car. God can be cruel, she thought. Vicky restarted her car and drove off. But where to? She had no place to go. She never really did. She just kept trying new things in her life as if that might do it— men, jobs, all the same.

The traffic on Broadway was wonderfully thick, like chilled honey. She put off deciding where to turn. Just be part of a crowd. A few blocks from the apartment, when Vicky saw a long line at the Peter Norton Symphony Space— and parking room right in front as if the universe had deemed it to be—she pulled in. She stepped into line behind a short, elderly woman with a plastic scarf on her head even though there was no sign of rain. Vicky said nothing but hoped the line would not move fast.

"Do you think we'll make it?" the elderly woman asked Vicky.

"I don't know. What's this for anyway?"

"You don't know what you're in line for?"

"A ticket."

"Sold out. This is for cancellations to *Heaven*."

Vicky looked up to the marquee and saw indeed it was for the popular new play, *Heaven*. The performance was still two hours away. She had something to do for two hours—and more if she got in. Afterwards, if she still felt grim, she consoled herself with the idea she could always jump off the George Washington Bridge.

For the first thirty minutes Vicky kept staring at her shoes. Her feet were real, she thought, made from calcium from old cows and Tums. She thought of all the shoes she had, from the first ones her mother must have bought her to these white, scuffed running shoes. Now her shoes had nowhere to run. Her feet could go on no longer.

"Vicky?" she heard a voice say, and looked up to see Bruce, his breath smelling of mint he was so close.

"What're you doing here?" she said.

"I should ask the same. I was on my way to get something to eat when I saw your car and then here you are in line!" he said with some emphasis. "Are you here with someone, is that it?" Bruce then looked forward and back to see if there were some man approaching. "This photography thing was all made up so you could meet your lover?"

The woman with the plastic head scarf turned around and reevaluated Vicky.

"Don't be absurd," said Vicky. She noted Bruce's agitation. Indeed, he seemed jealous. That's a new one. Maybe he really cared. "Of course," she said, "you and I don't have much future, which you've made clear."

"We have plenty of future! Just because I don't subscribe to some religious dictum that says true love only exists when some minister or JP grants it to you doesn't mean I don't—"

"Forget it," she said. "You're right not to commit. The funeral thing didn't work. Happy? I was essentially thrown out. So you were correct. What's the point in marrying when I can't get anything right? I'll just move out."

"Is that the way you feel? That you don't get anything right?"

"My first husband," the elderly woman interrupted, "didn't get anything right. May he rest in peace. That asshole cost me three thousand dollars in funeral expenses."

Bruce pulled Vicky out of line, away from the woman, and he kept holding Vicky's hand. "I've, ah—" he started and stopped. "Christ," he tried again.

"What?"

"It's just that you're the world to me. Maybe you think it's stupid, but I haven't wanted to jinx that. I've known too many people get divorced, and I didn't want to be in those statistics."

"Ah. So my moving out won't be in the statistics. It doesn't count. You didn't fail."

"No, that's not it at all. Look at you and Jeffrey—you two divorced."

"He was never around. Marriage to me is getting in front of people and saying, 'I love her and will enjoy her, and I want all you to support us until one of us is thrown in the ground, stone dead.' And then you live each day like that, knowing it may be your last."

"You're serious," Bruce said. He looked off in surprise as if seeing a new grocery that he had never noticed before. "I've never thought of marriage that way. People who are married seem like they want out, but your way... I kind of like that."

"So you'll marry me?"

"I didn't say that, but, you know, can I get used to the idea?"

"Huh?"

"Please be patient a little longer. Stay with me. Let's go home."

Just as she was ready to say no, that she wasn't going to move from that spot until he was ready to proclaim what was right and come up with a wedding date, she felt a rain drop on her face, and then two more. One fat one hit Bruce right in the forehead. The elderly woman was correct about the rain. She turned to tell the woman so, but didn't see her.

It occurred to Vicky then that maybe her own instincts were not the best. Rain assessment, funeral photography, so much didn't work out. Like a blind dog, she needed a seeing-eye human. She stared at Bruce's face, his sweet, beautiful, dependable face, crinkled in expectation. "It's hard reaching the end of your thirties," she said.

She pulled Bruce off the sidewalk and led him to her car in the thickening rain. She and Bruce were reflected as a whole as well as celebrated in the energizing pixels of rain-drops on the rectangular lens of the windshield.

# He's Home

"Nikki, I'm home!" No answer.

"Nik?" I call again. Good. Now I can really surprise her. I take the bouquet of flowers from behind my back and enter our condo. The air feels stale, stiff, like a forgotten closet. No one has opened the back windows to the afternoon sun as I like, for the breeze. I notice, however, the living room is extraordinarily clean. I see vacuum marks in the rug, and the pillows are arranged on the couch and love seat perfectly, like a kiss. What a woman Nikki is. Maybe flowers aren't enough. If I could wrap a thousand butterflies into a rainbow, that's what I'd give her.

"Nikki, dear? Hello?" I call just to make sure and peek into the living room and bedroom to make sure she's gone. Good. I eagerly run into the kitchen for a vase, and again I'm stunned. The white porcelain sink gleams, as does the stainless steel rim. She scrubbed out my accident with the meatloaf and its red tomato stain, and the counter—the tile counter whose light blue diamond decorations remind me of my love's azure eyes—is so clean and smells of Pinesol. The ivory grout appears as it did when new. This woman must have been an army of cleaners. Even though I had my usual long day at the printing shop, she's been busier. She is so damn good to me. I am a lowly worm, and I should grovel in her shadow. She's Venus. A dozen bouquets, two hundred shoulder and foot rubs, and a thousand cats purring like a symphony wouldn't be enough. Quick, I remind myself. I take the crystal vase down from the cupboard, the vase my late mother gave me, and I arrange the flowers. The head of the single yellow rose nestles like a angel among the lilies and baby's breath. I add water and dash into the dining room with the arrangement. The center of the table is perfect for it. She even put a doily here, as if she were waiting for the vase. She'll see the flowers first thing. I hope she's surprised.

I'm too impatient. I just want to see her face. It's sensuous and framed, like the Madonna, by long auburn hair. I love the way she kisses. She's so damn patient with me.

I'm feeling stupidly sensitive—old or something. But fifty is not old. Just fifteen years older than she. Hell, just relax. What should I do? Read the mail. I can read the mail without her telling me not to read the mail before dinner.

As I read the mail, I feel thirsty. Is that what I feel? I'm trying to get a hold of this new-age, new-man kind of thing. Listen to my inner being. Don't squelch it. Be sensitive. I fart, but that's okay—she's not here to say she felt the room move and make some joke about the Richter scale. I'm thirsty, hoping that's all it is.

I return to the kitchen, but I don't find a glass in the dishwasher. Everything has been put away. With a glass from the cupboard, I drink. What can I do for her in return? The garbage. I'll take out the garbage. But beneath the sink, the pail is empty with a new, white garbage bag. Wow. Maybe she's home after all, outside.

I go to the back door. "Nikki?"

I listen. "Nik?"

Nothing. "Are you out here?"

I notice a dog, a long-nosed golden retriever, pause from his sauntering down the street to consider me. What's he thinking? Perhaps I've ruined his doggie solitude or perhaps he's just mulling, "There's a silly human who's lost his mate again." Except how does a dog know I'm calling for my mate? I could be calling my pet Chihuahua or even a pet eagle that comes on call. If I had an eagle, I could have it peck that dog's eyes out.

"Maggie? Here kitty, kitty, kitty." I'm not so worried about the black, loose-bellied cat. I've had the cat twelve years now, two years more than I've known Nik, and the cat knows to stay away from dogs. The cat will show up later.

I return inside.

It occurs to me she probably did not actually take the garbage out but hid it to save herself steps. I look in the hall closet. It has to be here somewhere. She loves hounding me about the garbage. It's a sore point with us. I usually stand my ground, saying I'll do it later. I hate her asking me, nagging me—it bugs me! She knows that. I know, too, that saying I'll do it later annoys her. It shows, however, I'm not ruled by her whims or commands. Our marriage counselor called my response "passive aggressive." Screw that. Besides, how good could the counselor be if he had such a deep tan and athletic build and talked about "marriage is like swimming?" It's not like swimming, unless you include drowning. It's more like nude boxing. With words, you hit each other's tender spots a lot, but now and then you wrap your arms around each other and do the big nasty. Our counselor was too off-center for me. Flaky. I refused to see him again.

The mail hums—literally it's got a sound—and I shuffle through it quickly, listening, throwing the mail on the ground until I realize the sound's in my head. The hum grows into a soft scream. I notice my mouth is open. I'm screaming. What the hell's wrong with me?

I leave the mail and go to the bedroom. The bed is made perfectly, its thick cotton cover like a shroud, not a wrinkle. We bought the bedcover in Japan on our one-and-only trip. The cover's been in the closet because she hates the dragon motif. "Nik? Nik? I love you, Nik." And I truly do. I joined Scientology because you did, remember? I named my row boat after you, too. If I had a power boat, it'd have "Nikki" boldly across its stern.

I run into the bathroom, and the tiles here, too, glare right in my face. The floor is spotless, the air, sharp with Clorox. The whole bathroom smiles in a rictus. It's then I notice the open shelves in the corner have nothing—all her Kotex and bargain-discount toilet paper gone. So, too, are the towels. I open up the medicine cabinet—her side is empty, gone. I can hardly breathe. My vision blurs. It's like my stomach has become a fist and hits all my organs from the inside.

"Nik? Nik?" I rip open the shower curtain, pulling it too hard. The aluminum rod hammers down. Nik's not behind the shower curtain, a place I found her once in hiding. I jump up and down on the rod, mashing sections into road kill—goddamn thing shouldn't fall down.

I catch my face in the medicine cabinet mirrors, three faces of Steve. Steven. I say Steven and people call me Steve. Damn Americans. They don't know what it's like for an immigrant. I pay taxes—ten thousand dollars last year. I'm a good citizen.

The mirrors, however, make me look like something you'd see on a matchbook cover, one of those sketch drawings, below which says, "You too can learn to draw!" I'm not a cartoon. Men with short beards are not cartoons. I take the flattened rod and smash the mirrors and pull down the empty shelving unit. The noise comforts me until I think God damn it, she didn't leave. Just check her closet.

I dash to her closet. Nothing's there. She's left me! Why? Just last night she made me meatloaf, cabbage, and Rice Crispy treats, my favorite foods. I told her I loved her. I thanked her. I hugged her. I'm modern. I know she needs it. We even almost made love. Okay, so I was a little tired, but a fifty-year-old man can get tired. I said that's what you get for marrying a sweet old man. "Sweet old men don't hit," she said, but I didn't hit her—I'm not some monster. That was misplaced anger like the counselor said. I said I was sorry. Something just overcomes me, I'm sorry, I just don't mean to get so mad. It's like that shower rod, it's one of those things. Give a guy a break.

The scream again. I won't cry—I won't permit it. I cannot let this happen. "Nik! What the hell do you want?"

I run into the kitchen and throw open the tall, narrow cabinet. I shove cans and jars out of the way as if I'm searching for something, but that's not the point. I make it so the shelves hold nothing. I am nothing. God is nothing. The jars of Ragu spaghetti sauce crack open on the floor like gourds or heads. I thrust my hands into its indifferent red juice and fling it about the kitchen. Red splatters against the white cabinet doors. I've cut my hands on some glass, and my red mixes with Ragu's. I've created a mess, I'm sorry. This isn't fair.

I'm crying now. This isn't fair. I wish I could crush her throat like a white eggshell.

A black flash flicks by—the cat. "Maggie, I'll kill you!" But I can't move beyond a stumble, and she darts out the open back door. I watch her as she paws up the wall and over.

# *Engaging Ben*

S arah strode in from the kitchen to the dining room table and set down the hard black mug of coffee with emphasis in front of Ben. She eyed him and turned without saying anything.

"Good morning," Ben said as she went around the corner, her long dark hair flying. He paused for a response, heard nothing, and added, "Join me?" It was then he heard the bedroom door close. What did he do now? He'd been up only a few minutes, what could he have possibly done?

If Ben had to critique his fiancée, Sarah would definitely lose out in the communications department. She always turned things into dramas. As he sipped his coffee, he tried to ascertain what he could have possibly done to offend her now. If he had to give her an overall rating lately, she would get only five stars out of ten. When they fell in love, she was easily an eleven, but as the wedding approached, she was losing points fast. As much as he hated the thought, if she went down another star, he might have to break off the engagement altogether. Maybe it would wake her up to her problem.

Part of the problem, perhaps why she became so moody, was that she had become obsessed with food lately. She was not fat, just a little bigger, as if someone had blown too much air into her arms and legs. That must have played on her subconscious somehow. "Carbohydrates," he told her at breakfast one morning, holding up his single Pop-Tart, "become simple sugars quickly. Too many simple sugars at once turn into fat. People should watch how many carbohydrates they eat."

"Then don't eat the damn thing," she said, clearly not connecting that he was talking about her. As if to disagree with him further, she showed him the government pyramid on the back of the Cheerios box that said that people are supposed to be eating more carbohydrates and much less fat.

"The government doesn't know anything about food," Ben told her. "If they did, if they cared about what went in things, they wouldn't let people sell hot dogs."

"Breads," she said pointing to the box. "We're supposed to be eating more breads, grains, and vegetables and much less meat." In fact, as the cook, she had cut out steak from their diet the month before and replaced it with tofu and toast. Ben had deducted a star from her rating for that alone.

"I don't consider tofu a bread or grain—and anything that white and jiggly can't be a vegetable."

"What're you saying?" she said defensively. "That I don't satisfy you?" Sex. That was another matter.

Ben now stood and went into the kitchen to get more milk for his coffee. Their dinner plates from last night, with bits of mashed potato and green beans still on their plates, still sat on the counter, and many empty used glasses stood in the sink. He had cooked for once, and she was supposed to clean—that was the deal.

But he knew, too, she wasn't going to change. She had always been a slob. When they first started dating, and they were both in grad school, he found her apartment amusing in the way she had spiral notebooks, Norton anthologies, research on James Joyce, and other various bindings in piles all over her living room like lily pads on a pond. She laughed when the first thing he did upon entering her apartment was straighten a photograph of sunflowers on the wall. Now that they were living together, he could not stand how her underwear lay scattered like soiled tissues across their bedroom, how her tea cups could be found on shelves and tables throughout their rented Santa Rosa house, and how the newspaper would manage to explode from its rubber band each morning, sections to be found in disarray in each room where she had read them.

But that was Sarah. After he had sold his one-and-only screenplay two years out of grad school, and they had moved to Santa Rosa in Northern California, he had hired a maid to pick up after her. Life had been good.

Now that he hadn't sold anything in three years, he recently let the maid go and figured he had to let the house be a mess versus cleaning it himself or he would never get his story about a reanimated gladiator off the ground. Thoughts of his script made him wince. The gladiator had been found frozen beneath the Coliseum in Rome. Ben still hadn't solved how the Romans froze him or why he stayed frozen or how he was able to come back to life, but those were details he could get to if he could only concentrate. If this wedding thing didn't keep interrupting.

Sarah had demanded on New Year's Eve that he choose a wedding date, and he suggested one five years hence, laughing. She was serious. This year or never. Heck, if it were that important, he would choose July. Everyone was on hiatus in Hollywood in July, so even if his career sprang back to life, nothing would be happening then. He hadn't planned on selling a pitch, as he did, however; the producers wanted a finished script by July.

Dirk—that's what Ben's fictional anthropologists had affectionately nicknamed the gladiator—had gone nuts finding that nearly the entire population of Rome was now Christian. Dirk escaped. As deacon after priest after bishop was found brutally murdered, it became clear who the gladiator was really after: the Pope. Only an American baby sitter named Sally Renfield—on vacation in Rome—could save the Pope.

After Ben finished his coffee, alone at the dining room table, he stepped into their messy bedroom and heard the shower running. No point in finding out what's wrong now. He moved into his office at the end of the hall in the T-shirt and dirty khakis that he'd worn the day before and went to work.

"Ben, honey," said Sarah at his door late that afternoon. "Do you know where the chocolate-covered graham crackers went? I bought them yesterday."

"What?" he said. His stomach grumbled. He had missed lunch because he had been concentrating so hard. "I'm working. I just had Sally jump into a manhole, and these creatures that I call the Morlocks are about to get her—if Dirk the Gladiator doesn't."

"You can't call them the Morlocks."

"Why not? It has a good ring to it."

"That's the name of the creatures in H.G. Wells's novel, *The Time Machine.*"

"Oh," he replied, now remembering vaguely that he had read the book in college. "The producers won't know—they never read."

"But maybe they saw the movie. Why do you have these things in a gladiator movie anyway?"

"It puts her in peril."

"Can't the gladiator do that by himself?"

He only looked at the ceiling. Such help he didn't need.

"Can't you call them something similar sounding?" she then said. "Like the Dreadlocks?"

"That's a hair style! You can't have creatures named after a hair style! That's something your friend Val would say."

"So now you criticize Val," she said.

"She's strange. Her ideas are borderline."

"And having Morlocks in a gladiator movie isn't?"

Couldn't he just be left alone? "Don't you have a class to teach?" he said.

"Ben. That's Tuesdays and Thursdays. Can't you ever remember? Today's Wednesday."

Which reminded him of another star that she lost. Lack of drive. She seemed perfectly content to teach just two extension classes in literature two evenings a week at Santa

Rosa Community College. Was she just going to sail through life as if it were some afternoon tea?

"So where are the crackers?" she asked.

"I ate them."

"You ate three pounds of crackers in a day?"

"I was hungry."

"You threw them out, didn't you?"

"No." Truth was, he did. Three more pounds of carbohydrates she didn't need. Why couldn't she be thin again and enjoy sex like she once did? He remembered when he absolutely needed her. He had been like a diabetic in need of insulin—he could hardly breathe or get her clothes off fast enough if more than 24 hours had gone by—and she would grin knowing his need.

Now she had *Brides* magazine to read, a list of guests to invite that changed daily, and dinners to try at various hotels—dinners during which she ate mostly carbohydrates. Sex was only once a week at best. How to get her back to what they had?

"Asshole," she said and turned on her heel.

That did it for him. He couldn't get married—not now. "These constant interruptions for stupid things," he began.

"Stupid?" she said, returning.

"How can we marry?" he said. "I can't—not in July, at least."

"What is stupid is how you've been recently," she spouted. "What's your problem? You've been on me for weeks, and it's driving me nuts. What do you have, that Peter Pan Syndrome? Grow up already." And with that, she left. Right down the hall. Right out the door. She did not return that night.

As she drove in Ben's BMW on the 101 toward San Francisco, Sarah wondered how she could get involved with such an obsessive guy as Ben. The fact was that biology is indeed destiny. Many of her friends—even Val, the so-called arch feminist from her Women in Literature class—had married by twenty-six. Val dropped her last name in favor of her husband's, Jerry Huffington. "I like it better than mine," Val said. "And I don't want a kid with a hyphen in his name."

Fact was, even though Val might have had time for dating and marriage in graduate school at USC, Sarah had not. She had planned specifically not to get involved while she was a student. As fun as they were, men were just too damn time-consuming and uncontrollable.

Sarah, however, began noticing babies: in backpacks on line at lunch, on the library lawn by Tommy Trojan, even in commercials on TV. Val, a breath after her "I Do," became pregnant—and Sarah felt a pang of envy. Sarah's younger sister Joey, in Massachusetts, had a two-year-old, Hastings, and kept telling Sarah how fun kids were.

"Have one before you get too old," said Joey. "Eggs start getting old at thirty."

Human eggs have a shelf life? Sarah was twenty eight then. In a previous century, one with gladiators in it, Sarah would have had four or more children at this age. Then again, in a previous century, women would not have debated deconstructionism, let alone analyzed something as rich and complex as *Finnegan's Wake*.

Despite Sarah's love of books, however, baby faces poked their way into her consciousness. She noticed how diapers were right across from the cereal at the supermarket. She saw as she ran around the track that some women ran pushing a special three-wheeled stroller with their babies in front. And where were the children in most of Chekhov's stories?

The hormones were definitely getting the better of her. Reproduction was a powerful call. She was ready. Her eggs were ready.

And then she met Ben. "It's all about timing," she told him cryptically one day. He asked what that meant, but she dropped the topic.

He was different from her previous lovers, which she arrayed like a set of bowling pins in her mind. There was Eddie, the snake handler. Freddie, the hair dresser. Alphie, the garage mechanic. Ben was the first man she dated in years that didn't have an "ee" sound in his name, that had had an education, and didn't have a funny smell to his hands after work. This, too, must have been her hormones dictating. Her set of genes wanted the best possible match.

She saw herself do things she had never done before. For instance, she shaved Ben's face as they took a bath together once, intrigued at the sound the razor made as it cut the thick tiny black hairs, amazed she wanted him so much. He had a wonderful, taut body. He was so boyish and bold, he could have been a fireman.

She shaved her own armpits, too, something she thought she'd never do. She loved playing with Ben's penis, watching it grow. How weird to walk around with such a thing all day. These thoughts made her feel like she had valence, a need to combine with other atoms.

"You're so lean and muscled," she had said to him the first time they made love.

"That's from my bike riding," he replied. "Do you like riding?"

She sat on top of him and guided him into the spot. "Let's just say I like riding."

Logic won out, though. Ben had a lot of logic. They had to get their careers going first, he said, before starting a family. He didn't want children until they were married. He was in the Filmic Writing Program at USC, and he only wanted to write a great script. Which he did. He sold it a few years after they graduated. His career was going.

Then he wanted to write another script. This second script had him so self-absorbed, it's as if he had changed the rules, so she pushed for something she never thought she needed: marriage.

July it would be. But Ben started getting funny. His first script had been about a young man falling for a Japanese woman and how their cultures kept them apart. This new script about a gladiator—what was that about?

He spoke of neatness, but he started leaving his shower towels on the floor, his side of the bed unmade, and his plates at the table. Did he assume this was women's work?

She noticed, too, how he was becoming obsessive about many things. He now always buttered his toast from left to right. He drank his beer in twelve swallows—an ounce a swallow, he said. He lined up all his shoes in his closet in an order of darkness to lightness. She noticed when they made love now—always on a Saturday night because that's the only time he seemed receptive—he always started at her feet and worked his way up—never varying.

My god, would he computerize their lives? And he had become so critical lately. It was like living with a walking reviewer. Whatever room they would be in, he could point out something she had done wrong. "Are bras supposed to be hung from your bureau's knobs? I think not. Is the hallway where the broom should be left? No."

How could she marry him? But her parents had already booked a hotel, relatives had been contacted, and every girlfriend had given her at least one copy of *Brides*. Everyone was expectantly waiting for the invitations. Her eggs were saying do it, do it. Then Ben threw on the proverbial straw that broke her back: he had to go throw away her crackers. Fuck him!

Val, in San Francisco on business, had called Sarah earlier that morning,. Stanford had actually flown Val out for an interview in the English department, and she was also checking out Berkeley. Sarah fled to Ben's car—it had gas—and hoped she could still find Val, an hour and a half away in San Francisco.

"Oh for Christsakes, Sarah," said Val with a laugh as they sat in the hotel bar. "Do you live in a dream world? All men are babies."

"But you and Jerry—"

"Jerry's a baby, too."

Sarah ripped open the tiny, silver-sealed bag of pretzels with her teeth, just as a waitress in a short dress delivered their drinks. Val glanced at the woman's thin, toned legs and whispered, "Five more years and a baby, and let's see what they look like."

The woman deposited Sarah's Pinot Noir and Valerie's Chardonnay. Sarah glanced around at the elegantly framed prints on the dark wood and the Waterford glasses above the bar. Stanford had put Valerie up at the Fairmont. Not bad. And Val in her blue suit and designer blouse looked professional. What happened to the woman who wore the Indian-print skirts and tight T-shirts?

"I don't mean I don't love Jerry," added Val, "but it's pretty damned hard. Those pretzels, by the way—a lot of carbs."

"The government food pyramid says—"

"Fuck the government. Notice how people are looking like Fuji blimps? The government wants fat people. Helps the economy."

Sarah was too impatient to go on with this. "Should I leave Ben or what?"

"Marry the bastard. Especially if he's the least bit contrite."

"I'm not going back there."

"Stay here if you want."

"Ben has an alarm on his watch which he's set for nine fifty-two p.m. When it goes off, he marches to the bathroom, and he gets ready for bed. That's so he can wake up at four fifty-two a.m. to write a gladiator movie. I'm a passenger on a very weird and regulated train."

"We all are!" Again Val laughed. "Jerry washes his socks in the bathroom sink every night. Then he picks between his toes and flicks the schmutz."

"Can't life be more interesting?"

"If you look at Salinger—"

"Not J.D. Salinger and bananafish again," said Sarah.

"Why do you think I wrote a book about the darkness in J.D. Salinger's fiction? Gave me something to do besides change diapers and hear about how tough the graphic design business is for Jerry. I published the book, and here I am. Life's great—even if Jerry's a jerk. Ben's a jerk. They're all that way."

They ordered dinner there in the bar, fish and chips. Val drank her Chardonnay down as if it were a shot of tequila. That's the Val Sarah knew. "Listen," said Val leaning in. "What do we all want? Help, right? Help me through this damn lonely world and listen to me. Help me on this planet where the nightly news is simply an affirmation of the daily evil around us. An immigrant is raped with a toilet plunger. A child is kidnapped by a stranger and found dead two days later. Princess Di is chased by paparazzi and dies in a car crash. And, oh yes, the fire department saved a kitten from a tree. News at eleven."

"At least they get something nice in," said Sarah.

"I mean, it's so easy to be cynical these days. And husbands don't help that. Their needs are different from ours. It's as if they're on some sort of scoreboard, always looking to see if their name is going higher or lower. They want to be adored—don't we all? As they get older, they pine for younger women. The rules of this world are this: experience what you can. Don't expect a lot. That's why I say, marry. Have kids. Children remind you of what's good, what it was like before we knew better. If Ben doesn't make a good husband, don't focus on what could or should have been—at least you've been living life. This is what I've learned being an English major," she said, smiling and leaning back again. "I know you know it, too."

Later, up in Valerie's room, Sarah stared out at the city, whose hills were suggested by the way the lights looked like candles caught on frozen waves. She figured that each light represented at least one person. How many of those lights were really gray? How many wanted to be extinguished?

Val emerged from the bathroom in black pants and a T-shirt. She actually looked better than in grad school. "Ready?" she asked Sarah. Sarah nodded.

They grabbed a cab out front, which lurched up and down a few hills, and were driven to a club the concierge at the front desk suggested, the Marina Club. It offered a disc jockey and dancing and a nighttime view of Alcatraz. This felt so illicit to Sarah, that she felt hopeful, actually. It didn't take long for her to be asked for a dance.

Ben told himself Sarah would be back in five minutes. He was even relieved, thinking she would cool herself off. An hour later, after she had not returned, he wondered where she could have possibly gone. She had never done anything like this before. Why would she do this? Maybe he should think like her. No. He didn't know how to be insane. Except she really wasn't insane—just illogical.

As he tried to get back to writing, all he could think about was where would she go? The movies? A restaurant? Someone's house? He could not write. He had a sinking feeling he may have been too flippant about the wedding with her. By dinner, he knew that was a definite. Sarah was right in that he had been "on her" recently, being too critical. But getting engaged and living together wasn't a warm-up for life. It was life. She, if anyone, was the Peter Pan, playing around. Sarah had so much potential. Life was too short to coast.

As he made himself a peanut butter and jelly sandwich for supper, he really began to worry. Was she leaving him? This was not like her. Ever since Val married and moved to Boston, Sarah did not have any close friends nearby. Sarah did not spend a lot of time with other people; no one took up her time or attention as Val once had. So where would Sarah go? Sarah spoke to her sister a lot, but Joey also lived in Massachusetts. Sarah wouldn't be crazy enough to fly there, would she?

He made himself a cup of coffee and sat at the dining room table, eating the sandwich and washing it down with the hot black beverage. He thought he heard her. He turned and saw nothing, not even their cat, Hairball. His anticipation made him remember how she turned to him the other day, a smile on her face, as she worked on a crossword. "What's a seven-letter word for constipated?" she asked. Costive, she came up with a moment later, a word he had never heard of. God, he's been costive, emotionally, he realized. He's been very difficult to live with. Sarah was just an innocent, someone whose needs were simple. She loved reading and teaching literature. She loved doing the Sunday crossword. Was it wrong to want someone you loved to do even more? That question told him something: He loved her.

Okay, she did not push herself or clean up after herself, but she could take some damn rose that he bought at a stop light and fawn over it, really love the gesture. She planted artichokes in the garden just for him. She would notice when his shoelaces were wearing out before he did and buy him a new pair. Best of all, she would read everything he wrote, and even if she found little corrections to be made, she always loved his work. She treated him as if there were no one else in the world she cared for. Why did he poison that by telling her no marriage? He really loved her. He had to tell her all this. He had to tell her this tonight.

He combed Sarah's desk and dresser for any clues. Nothing. He took her bras off the knobs and put them neatly in a drawer. He looked carefully through all the thumb-tacked notes on the bulletin board by the hall phone. Still nothing.

Under the dining room table, he found the backpack in which she carried her schoolwork, and inside was her Day Timer. Ben methodically went through her address file to look for familiar names. He recognized two women teachers from the college and called them each. They had not seen Sarah since the evening before and found his tone worrisome. They kept asking if anything was wrong with her. "No," he said, varying what came next. "She's been so busy with wedding plans, maybe she forgot about dinner."

By nine o'clock, Ben was getting so desperate, he called Val in Boston. Jerry answered sleepily.

"Hi, Jerry," said Ben. "It's me, Ben. Sarah's fiancé?"

"Huh?... It's after midnight."

"It's been a few years since we talked."

"Can we talk in the morning?"

"Sarah and I are getting married. Val probably told you."

"Oh, yes. Congratulations."

"Is Val there? I need to talk with her."

"Val's in your neck of the woods. Didn't you know?"

"She is? Where exactly?"

The man who asked her to dance wore canvas tennis shoes, black with a white stripe. Sarah had been sitting with Val eating some peanuts when the barrette she had been fingering like a rosary under the table had dropped to the floor among the peanut shells. On her knees, she saw the tennis shoes approach her. She also found her barrette.

"Miss," said a strong voice, with the hint of a Southern lilt. She looked up to see a boyish-looking man with a cleft chin and a bright smile extending his hand. He looked a few years younger than herself and wore a beret. "Care to dance?" he asked.

"I can't," said Sarah. "My friend and I are—"

"Go ahead!" said Val. "Live a little."

"No, really, I'm about to—"

"Sarah," said Val. "This is the tonic you need."

"My name's Jimmy," said the man as they approached the dance floor, the bass from the music thumping in a pulsating beat. The music drove the changing colored lights and the movements of men and women in their summer shorts. When Sarah glanced over to Val, she saw that a man in a crew cut had already joined her, taking Sarah's stool.

"You looked so pretty," said Jimmy. "I just had to ask for the dance."

"Thank you," said Sarah, not knowing really what else to say. "I'm Sarah." He took her hand, and she felt the calluses on his palm. "What do you do for a living?" said Sarah.

"I work for the city. I repair the cable car cables."

"That's specialized."

"Rice-a-Roni. A San Francisco treat," he said with a laugh. "I saw that commercial so much as a kid, maybe that's what drew me to this city and the job. Been here five years now. And what do you do?"

"An English teacher," she said as he guided her under his arms. He really did have good rhythm.

"Heck," he said. "Never was really great at English."

"Ain't nothin' to it."

"You're smart. I like that!"

She smiled. "Thanks." As they danced, she thought of Ben. What was he doing right now? It was after ten, so he probably was sleeping. Nothing was going to throw off his rhythms, even her. It would really take until the morning for him to notice she was not back. But would it matter? Better to make a clean break now, rather than have months or even years of their mismatched temperament working at each other. As for babies, all she needed was a little sperm. Where was the best place to get that?

"You really are pretty," said Jimmy.

Ben ran out the door, consumed with one image: Sarah. Val would surely give her terrible advice. He had to get there fast. He stood disoriented for a moment, staring where his red BMW should have been. Sarah must have taken it—something Freudian there, surely. Good. Maybe she needed him, after all.

He fumbled for his keys—did he put her Honda keys on his pocket knife key ring? No. Her keys were in the house. He was so flustered that he kept putting the wrong key in the front door lock. All he could think of was how he was losing precious seconds. At last he opened the door, found her spare keys in the nightstand where he left them, and dashed to her dented Honda. He backed it up so fast, he scraped the brick wall that ran the length of the driveway, creating sparks. He told himself to worry about the damage later. Just get to San Francisco.

A block later, the car was dead. He looked to the gas gauge. Empty. That's why she took his car.

He ran breathlessly back to their garage, grabbed the gas can for the lawn mower, and laughed when he felt it was still mostly full. He had some luck after all.

The gas was enough to get him to the gas station. He was on the road shortly after that. He concentrated with such intent that he drove over 80 miles per hour the whole way, maneuvering gracefully like a bird in a tail wind. He gave the correct change on the Golden Gate Bridge to the person in the tollbooth, and he was in the city in under an hour—a record for him. He vaguely knew where the Fairmont was; he made it there directly.

He leapt from the car, more consumed than ever. He told the valet to keep the car nearby, as he might need it in a few minutes.

The desk clerk, a young woman in her early twenties, would not give the room number to Val's room, but, after asking him to spell her last name, would only confirm she was a guest there. She had him use the house phone. The operator for the house phone made him spell, all over again, Val's last name. No answer.

He ran back to the desk. This time the concierge was there, and Ben asked where Val Huffington might be. He didn't know. Ben described Sarah, what she had been wearing and adding she had "the greenest, most beautiful eyes you've ever seen."

"Yes, I remember," said the concierge. "I told them about the Marina Club. Maybe they went there."

Out front, the valet had not even moved the Honda yet. He was having a smoke. Ben handed him a five, jumped in the car, and hurried toward the Marina.

The red neon of the "Marina Club" sign was cradled by the masts of luxury sailboats on either side, a full moon reflecting off the water. To the right, like a reminder of man's imperfection, stood Alcatraz with lights on its crumbling prison and water tower. Ben left the car with the valet and dashed toward the door, only to be stopped by a doorman the size of a trawler.

"What, is there a cover charge?" Ben asked.

"I don't like your attitude already," said the doorman, a full five inches taller than Ben, and, from the girth of his arms, a man who clearly spent time working out.

"So how much?" said Ben, taking out his wallet.

"First of all, there's a dress code here. You don't make it." This was said as the man flagged a young couple past—both of them in shorts, sandals and Hawaiian shirts. The woman, in fact, wore black Spandex shorts so tight every man within fifty feet was staring.

"What kind of dress code is that!" Ben spouted.

"That's *style*. And they're not wearing dirty jeans or a plain white T-shirt and homeless shoes like you are." His tennis shoes had little holes. Sarah had wanted to throw them out, but he insisted on keeping them. His lucky writing shoes were very comfortable.

"These aren't jeans!" said Ben, unintendedly pointing to his knees made dirty from gardening. "They're khakis. Ernest Hemingway wore khakis!"

"Should I know him?" said the doorman. "Does he dance here?"

"Let me in! Here's twenty!"

"Even if I let the pants go, which I would if they were clean or shorts, you have a problem with the shoes and shirt. Sorry. Come back better dressed next time."

All Ben could do was emit a guttural sound and step away. He noticed the silhouettes of sailboat masts around him, crosses in the night. He turned to stare at the white wooden building knowing Sarah was in there. Changing colored light—red, yellow, green—spilled from a picture window onto the white railings and nearby boats. A heavy, pounding sound emanated, too, emphasizing the dance beat.

When the doorman was dealing with new people, Ben ran to the side, away from the doorman's view and around to the window. In front of the window, Ben was able to look right onto the dance floor. Ben stood like a fly in a web, stuck. He focused from face-to-face. At last he saw Sarah, dancing with some geek in tennis shoes and a beret. Ben pounded on the window. "Sarah! Sarah!"

All Ben managed to do was draw the attention of a security guard outside, an older, gray-haired man in a tan uniform with thick, dark shoes and a flashlight.

"You can't do that," said the man, waving the light in Ben's eyes. "The entrance is in the front."

Ben focused on the man's shoes. "I'll give you forty dollars for those shoes!" said Ben.

"These?" said the man, incredulous. "They're orthopedic. Cost me nearly seventy dollars."

Ben pulled five twenties out of his wallet. "Here's a hundred, and I'll give you these tennis shoes in trade, too."

"Hell," said the man, starting to take off his shoes. "Wait till my wife hears this one."

As Ben jammed a foot into one shoe, he felt something odd and pulled out a Dr. Scholl's footpad. He yanked out the pad from the other shoe, too, slipped on his new footwear, and ran with a clomp down the dock as he saw a couple head toward the boats. The man, who looked like a clean-cut CIA agent on vacation, wore a green, Izod shirt, the object of Ben's attention.

"Excuse me!" Ben gasped. They stopped. Ben ran to them.

"Hi," said Ben. "This may sound ridiculous, but the Marina Club has a dress code—anything but white T-shirts apparently—so I was wondering if I could buy your shirt you're wearing. Twenty dollars?"

"We're busy," said the man.

"Forty," said Ben.

"How much for mine?" said the woman, in her twenties, who wore a stretchy low-cut halter-top.

"Jane," said the man to the woman. "Don't be ridiculous."

"I love spontaneity," said the woman and promptly removed her top, leaving her in a black bra. "Here, let's swap. I can use your T-shirt for a rag."

Ben eagerly removed his T-shirt and put on the halter-top—which was very tight on him. He looked alien with all his chest hair.

"Thanks!" Ben shouted and clomped off. Back at the head of the dock, Ben realized he still had to deal with his pants. He pulled out his pocketknife key chain, flicked open the blade, and cut off his pants legs haphazardly into shorts. The dirty spots on his knees were gone.

The doorman laughed when he saw Ben. Even though there was a line now waiting to get in, he motioned Ben forward. A woman in line giggled and said to Ben, "You didn't make the callbacks to 'Nutcracker Suite' I bet."

The doorman said simply, "If you're that desperate, man," and thumbed Ben in.

Ben paid the $10 cover charge at a counter just inside and moved toward the music that grew louder with each step. He saw himself reflected in a mirror, a creature with protruding chest hair, funny shorts bulging on one side from his keys, and heavy industrial shoes. It occurred to him that under normal circumstances, he'd be highly critical of someone who looked like this. He had to smile. We all are complex creatures, aren't we?

The changing lights, the heavy beat, and the flow of people and waitresses disoriented him at first. He thought he saw Val, but she couldn't be that woman kissing a shorthaired man. Ben stepped closer just in case. The music had stopped. The D.J. was announcing a break.

"Val?" said Ben. She turned.

"Who are...." she started to say, and then recognition hit. "Ben? Ben, what are you—" And she started laughing. "I'm sorry, it's just— It's been a few years."

"Who's your friend?" Ben pointed to the man who he could now see was wearing a short-sleeved beige Marine uniform. The man's cap, with the Marine Corp globe on it, was folded inside his belt.

"Oh, ah... whoops." She turned to him. "What's your name?" she asked the man.

"I'm Alex," said the Marine standing and extending his hand to Ben. Ben shook it automatically. "Out for a little fun, are you?" Alex said, looking over Ben more closely.

"What's that mean?"

"Nothin'," said Alex. "I'm on leave tonight, shipping out tomorrow. I have no care in the world. Dress as Tinkerbell for all I care."

Ben paused, ready for trouble. He looked at Val. "Jerry didn't say you were divorced."

"I'm not."

Whether it was the house lights returning and people noticing Ben's clothes, or whether it was just a random lull in everyone's conversation, the room became an oasis of silence when Ben said, "I don't understand morality these days, I just don't. How can you make out with a man who's not your husband?"

"What?" said Alex, the Marine.

"Carpe diem," said Val.

"Semper Fidelis!" Alex shouted toward the ceiling. Ben, reacting to the sound—and assuming the Marine was looking for a fight—took action. Ben knew he had better be like a gladiator and get the Marine down on the first blow.

The man easily stopped Ben's fist with his large, beefy palm. Alex's steel, powerful fingers could have probably crushed Ben's fist if the man wanted to. That would have been the end to typing with that hand. Rather, Alex let go. "I didn't know, mister," said Alex. "And I don't date married women." The Marine gazed at the people staring at him as if he could own them. He turned, proud as a stag with huge antlers, and left.

All eyes were on Ben, who said, "E Pluribus Unum." It was the only Latin that came to mind. He also realized in that moment how he had to abandon his gladiator script—it wasn't true to him. He had to tie his own life more into things he knew—such as his life with Sarah.

Ben stood on his tiptoes to look for Sarah. He saw the man she had danced with, the man with the beret, moving toward the back, but no Sarah.

"Sarah?" Ben shouted, "Sarah!"

Sarah sat in a white molded plastic chair outside. Something had been happening to her. The lights. The music. The undulating bodies that had seemed so electric earlier began feeling claustrophobic. It's as if she couldn't take it in fast enough. Jimmy's face became a slash of a smile. An elbow from behind knocked her side, and someone stepped on her foot. The green light made everyone look sick, and wham went the music, the light changed to red, the music tempo went faster. Laughter seemed like knife blades. She felt as if she were falling from a roller coaster. "Ho!" someone shouted.

A sense of nausea had swept over Sarah. As she stopped to catch her breath, the smell of perfume mixed with sweat hit her and made her gag. "A shade of pain and then we die," was the only line she understood in the song, and then a big bass sound hammered at her.

"Cool!" shouted Jimmy. "Cool!"

Sarah could see the window. Window. She stumbled toward the picture window as if it were an exit. She had to stop this dizziness. There was a hand on her arm. Sarah turned.

"You okay?" Jimmy perhaps said, concern now on his face. She could only shake her head no. Sarah felt her knees give way as if they belonged to someone else, and all the legs and feet she saw coming at her seemed like pummeling, mashing spikes ready to chew into her.

As she was falling, she was thinking of Ben's phrase just last week as he was gathering clothes across the floor of their bedroom. "Simplify, simplify," he said. "Too much stuff can keep you from what you want."

108 • Engaging Ben

"Simplify?" she asked as hands clawed at her trying to save her.

When she opened her eyes, she saw the lights of the Golden Gate Bridge across the peaceful bay. The span of sodium lights held together the two quite different land masses, dark Marin and, after the Presidio, the bright glow of San Francisco. She felt the cool night air sweep over her. She sat in a white, molded chair on a deck over the water. Silent sailboats floated before her, docked in their berths, secure, safe.

"It can get hot in there," said a man in a yellow tie and a ring in his eyebrow.

"Sure can," said Jimmy, kneeling down. He had a child-like face, blond hair framing earnestness, a boy scout who had never heard a discouraging word and the skies were not cloudy all day. "Hey, darlin'," he winked. "You okay?"

"Yeah," she said. "I'm sorry."

"I'll let you two be," said Mr. Eyebrow Ring, who towered away. When the man opened the side door, the noise again bombarded her.

She straightened up, but her lightheadedness was not gone.

"Could you use a glass of water or something?" Jimmy asked.

"Water would be great," she said, not so much because she was thirsty, but because she really wanted to be left alone.

When Jimmy opened the door to go inside, she noticed the music had stopped and the lights inside were steady. The disc jockey must be between sets.

How did her life get so damn complicated? Ben would really be okay if he wasn't so programmed. He said you had to know what you needed and then don't let anything get in the way. "Plan your work and work your plan," was another one of his phrases. It was hard living with someone like that, though—you always felt lazy in comparison. Then again, until today, she always felt she was part of his plan.

Sarah could hear someone stepping onto the dock below her, a man and a woman. She bent forward to see. They were older, maybe in their fifties. As they walked, the man leaned over and kissed the woman, the light at the end of the dock silhouetting them. It wasn't a passionate kiss, just a simple peck, as simple as wind catching a sail. Ben gave Sarah those kind of kisses all the time—in the morning when he woke up, in the evening before they closed their eyes, at lunch when they'd meet. Recently, in fact, she asked him to stop the morning kisses because they always woke her up, like a happy dog in her face. But she now realized she missed those morning kisses. Would the evening and lunch kisses be gone now, too, because she had to go on this stupid night on the town?

Just as the door swung open by Jimmy with her drink she could hear the words, "Sarah? Sarah!"

A flash of adrenaline caught her. Could that be Ben? What would he be doing here?

"I didn't know if you liked bubbles in your water or not —" Jimmy began.

All Sarah could say as she moved past him was, "Excuse me a moment."

As if Sarah had some sort of force field, people parted easily as she walked through the crowd. Although she couldn't see him yet, the voice was so clearly Ben. Then she saw him, looking like a refugee from the Salvation Army. Everything about him said he needed her. Everything inside her said she needed him.

Ben saw her approach. "Sarah!" He rushed at her, but she did nothing, so he paused.

"I'm a fool in love," he said.

"Yes?"

"I had to get in to see you. I'm sorry for everything."

She ran to him, too, and they hugged and kissed. People clapped.

"So what're we going to do?" she asked, hopeful.

He simply held out his hand. She took it.

# Nike Had Nothing To Do With It

om Blanchard jogged underneath the five-fingered maple leaves in the dancing sunlight of the Maine woods. His feet smacked the hard worn dirt path, creating mini-clouds of dust, and the sun overhead flashed through the trees. Running was normally an energizing routine, but today he hoped it would drain his anger, well deserved as it was. His hands remained fists.

"I don't know how to say this," she had said, calmly buttering the English muffin, her favorite brand that he had bought from the mini-mart on Livermore Road. "But this isn't working out."

"What isn't working out?"

"Us."

He remembered looking up to see if she were teasing. While the last few weeks she had seemed a little distant and cool, he assumed it was the post-partum blues, which he had read about. Gwen had given birth to a beautiful baby girl, Stephanie, only three weeks ago, a year to the day after he had moved from Arizona to Maine to live with her. Tom and Gwen had met at his cousin's wedding in Portland. Their first kiss had come near a suit of armor at the Portland Museum of Art; they ate their first pizza together at Ribollita, an Italian café where he discovered her love of Portabello mushrooms. They first made love on a cot at his cousin's.

"Honey," he had said in his most calming voice while the baby slept in the next room. "Everything's perfect. We have a healthy baby, we're together, and life is good."

As she buttered her English muffin and shook her head, a tear escaped from one of her eyes. She was serious.

"We'll even get married soon, I promise," he added.

"Even? Even? Don't you see?"

"Let's get married *soon*."

"I don't want to marry. Not anymore."

As Tom jogged under the flickering leaves, his Nike shoes carrying him over the bumpy path, he remembered no, she had the word "you" in there, too. "I don't want to marry *you*."

"We can have the wedding you always wanted, in the pumpkin patch," he had urged, still calm, but starting to choke inside. The pumpkins were full, five acres of pregnant bellies.

"We can't. I'm in love with someone else."

"Who?"

"You don't want to know."

"*Who*? I changed my whole life for you! I left my friends, my family, my job, to be here with you. I have a right to know!"

She gave the gynecologist's name.

He laughed at that. "Sorry," he said, "but listen, your hormones are all out of whack. The body can do some pretty strange things."

"No. We're in love."

"It's true. The brain acts differently with so many hormones, and you're giving feelings to your doctor that he just doesn't need. It's like a schoolgirl's crush for her teacher— happens all the time, I'm sure. Sort of like lightning hitting a tree."

"No."

They talked for another fifteen minutes. Rather, he talked for another fifteen minutes, and she just cried silently. He had told her he loved Maine, even if there were no cacti. He loved their white, wooden house with its leaky faucets. He loved her. He even loved his new brokerage firm with guys who were teaching him to fish.

Tom stopped abruptly on the path because for a second he had seen only white, a flash. He felt dizzy. Maybe he would fall. This was just too weird. He punched the air like that guy in the movie, the boxer. What's his name? Names. What was his girlfriend's name? This was silly.

He sat under a tree. This was weird. How could he forget her name? Tip of the tongue thing. He knew it, just like... What was their baby's name? He felt lightheaded.

He looked out at where he was. The trees against the late afternoon light were majestic, giant pillars leading toward a hot white diamond. He saw a squirrel leap from one tree to another as smoothly as a stone skipping on a lake. Behind him was movement. He turned. A deer stood on stick legs and peered at him, not afraid, but curious, as if asking who is this guy? I'm... Now hold on here, I'm...

He couldn't remember his own name. He thought, *Now ain't that a funny thing?* He smiled. After a few more minutes, he stood and walked back on the path. He felt calm. He had forgotten where he had been headed, but he sensed that the path would take him where he needed to be. He told himself something was wrong, but what could be wrong when he felt perfectly fine?

As he approached the white two-story house, he noticed the house's green shutters picked up the color of the freshly mowed lawn. He breathed deeply the smell of the cut grass. He loved that. A bird called above him, and he looked up and saw a swath of blue landing on a limb. He was a man with luck.

When he walked into the kitchen, he found a woman slumped at the breakfast table, crying. He walked up to her and touched her shoulder compassionately without even thinking. She jerked aside, frightened. She gasped and held her arms up as if expecting to be hit. He looked at her, puzzled. Her eyes moved from terror to something more like that of the deer.

"I packed up your stuff and put it in your trunk," she said.

"What stuff?"

"Your clothes. Your camera and books. You really don't have a lot of stuff."

"Thank you," he said, assuming that was something really nice she had done. For the life of him, he couldn't think of a single thing he owned.

She stared at him. She stood and looked at him more closely.

"What?" he said. Behind her was a mirror. He noticed he was a man with white shoes, red jogging shorts, short brown hair, and a happy face.

"You're not mad?"

"Mad?"

"About us."

"Us? We're an us?" This pleased him to no end. He beamed. What a gorgeous creature she was, long blond hair, thin frame but with a paunch at the belly and wet spots at her breasts. She must be nursing. How wonderful! Isn't nature amazing?

"Are you alright, Tom?" she asked.

"Tom. I like that name. That's a good, simple name."

"Stop it!" she said.

"I'm sorry."

She stared at him more. "Are you okay?"

"I feel fine," he said. "I'm sorry, but what's your name again?"

"Stop fucking with me!"

"Oh." He stayed quiet. It was clear he was irritating her.

Her mouth hung open. "Tom?"

"You look so... upset?"

"Stop it! Stop it right now!"

He frowned. She was a very confusing woman.

"Your idea of a joke! This isn't funny!"

"I don't know any jokes." He sensed he should not do anything drastic, not even move. She snapped her fingers near his face, and he looked from one hand to the other, and it made him dizzy again, so he held up his arms defensively. Maybe she was going to hit him.

"What's wrong with you?" she said.

"Nothing."

"Maybe you had a stroke or something. This isn't right."

"Let me make you some breakfast. Food is a good thing, isn't it?"

"We've had breakfast!"

"We have?" He paused. He couldn't remember it. "How about lunch then? Have we had lunch?"

"I'm calling 911!" she shouted.

Those numbers sounded serious. She must really be mad. "I'm sorry if I've upset you," he said. "What can I do to help?" She probably just needed to get some fresh air. "Maybe you'd like to walk in the woods," he said. "It's beautiful out there right now."

"Where are we?"

He looked around. "This is the kitchen," he said.

"No, I mean what town?"

This puzzled him. He should know. "It's... It's... I'm sorry," he said. "It'll come to me in a minute."

"Tom, sit!" she said. He sat. "Tom, stand." He stood. He would do anything to show her there's nothing to be scared about. Thankfully, she was calm for several moments, just staring at him.

"I'm calling the doctor," she said. "Just sit." He did. He could see she was getting better, except her hands shook as she hurried to the phone out in the hall. He heard her press numbers and then say, "Frederick, it's me, Gwen."

Gwen? She turned her back to him and the rest of the conversation was mumbles, but it was a pleasing sound, like water over rocks. What a pleasant house this was, and right next to the perfect woods.

"Tom," she said, much more tentatively after she hung up, like someone trying to talk to another ready to jump off a bridge. "I've got to pack up Stephanie, but then we're going into town to the hospital, okay?"

"Hospital?" he said, concerned. "I think with a good lunch, you won't need a hospital."

"No, no, not me, but… the baby. It's time for Stephanie's checkup."

"Oh? Okay."

They drove toward Livermore Falls, and Tom smiled. As the images swept over the windshield, he felt this was all extremely special, as if he were in a movie. The houses looked like they were created as a set, painted perfectly, on green lawns and shaded by trees. The baby in the back cooed, and every time he looked at Gwen, Gwen made it a point to smile. She was clearly feeling better. All they needed was a drive.

As they drove under the arms of a great long set of trees, the sunlight bounced across the windshield like Morse code. Tom felt sleepy and he closed his eyes. He opened them as he was feeling himself shaken hard. She was shaking him. The car was now stopped on the side of the road, and the baby in the back was crying.

"Tom, you okay?" she shouted.

"What?" God, he was more fuzzy-headed than when he went to sleep. He must be really tired. He wondered what he had been doing. "Let me just sleep," he said.

"No, you were shaking violently like you were having a seizure," she said, holding him, hugging him. "Are you okay?"

"Just a little sleepy," he repeated. "Maybe you should feed the baby," he added, noticing her wet spots on her blouse.

"We've got to get you to the hospital!" she cried.

There she was all nervous and frightened again. What was her name again? She definitely looked unsteady. Maybe they'd better get to the hospital to look at her. "Yes," he said. "Let's get to the hospital."

Once there, the orderlies were all confused by her. She kept pointing to him, starting to cry again, and they didn't see it was she who was having the problems. "She's upset," he told the two orderlies who made him lie on a gurney. "I'll be better once I have a little sleep. Check her out first, please," he said.

"We will, sir," one of them told him.

A doctor who was short and who looked friendly approached. "I'm Dr. Needleman, remember me?" he said.

"No. Are you here to help her?" Tom pointed to his friend, the beautiful woman, who was just outside the doors, leaning into the back seat of the car.

"I've helped her already," the doctor explained.

"Maybe you didn't do a very good job, because she's really upset," said Tom. "She needs more help."

"No, I helped her with the baby."

"Oh!" said Tom, pleased. "Is that your baby?"

The doctor frowned, and he looked at Tom differently now, and he said more soberly, "No, that's your baby. I'm a gynecologist, and I just came to tell you that—"

"I thought you said you were a Needleman."

"Oh, Christ," said the doctor, throwing his hands in the air, at which point the beautiful woman approached with the baby sleeping on her shoulder, and she glared at the doctor's behavior. She came and took Tom's hand.

"As I was trying to explain," said Dr. Needleman, "I have contacted Dr. Stum, a top neurologist..." and the words went on like a waterfall. Tom could see the beautiful woman was agitated by this man in the way she kept telling him, "This is not the time." She was at Tom's side the whole while, holding his hand ever more tightly.

"I can't leave him now," she told the man.

"You don't have to stay with me," Tom said, reassuring her and looking at the doctor. "If he's going to look after you, go with him. I'll be fine."

"I'm not leaving you!" she shot back.

"I just want you better," Tom said.

The gynecologist backed off, hands in the air. She clearly didn't like the man. Tom wondered why.

Tom was moved into a room where a big machine was, and another doctor, with stylish gray hair, came to him and said, "I'm Dr. Stum. There's nothing to worry about here. I'm going to put you on the metal bed here, and it'll pull you into the center of the tube." The tube looked a lot like he was going to be buried. He was going to say no, but the beautiful woman—was this his wife?—looked so hopeful as he was being led to the metal bed that if this made her happy, he'd do it. He expected the chamber to fill with water, but it only buzzed. It wasn't so bad.

Later the beautiful woman nursed the baby at his side as he lay in a curtained off bay in the emergency room. He was mesmerized by the baby sucking at her breast, the baby's five little fingers gently stroking part of the rounded flesh. It looked right. It was the music of nature. Dr. Stum returned and said the MRI found no damage. No strokes. The beautiful woman seemed to know what all this meant because she smiled. The doctor explained that the light flashing through the leaves undoubtedly caused the seizures, much like a strobe light can to some people, but the seizures caused "minimal abnormality," mainly a temporary memory loss, much like what happens with electroshock therapy. Taking medication would prevent further seizures. Tom had to eat pills. If that would make her happy, he would do it.

Indeed, the medicine worked. Two weeks later, Tom woke up very early one morning with Gwen curled up at his side and her hand on his naked chest. He gently slipped out of bed and went into the bathroom. As he was taking a shower, he remembered what had happened just before he went jogging in the woods weeks earlier. At first he thought he was imagining it, but then he remembered details, such as the timbre of her voice as she said she did not want to marry him. He remembered how his stomach felt when she told him she was leaving him for the doctor. He remembered her saying his stuff was in his car's trunk.

After he tied his running shoes tightly, he hurried down to his car. His stuff was still there. Clearly, she was just humoring him lately. Fuck her. He slammed the trunk closed. After he backed the car up and thought of the long road to Arizona, he put the car into drive. He looked into the rear view mirror and saw the house one last time. Good-bye.

"Tom?" she said when she awoke, thinking he was in the bathroom. "I love you."

# High-Occupancy Vehicle

D arryl MacAnnany had not anticipated trouble. Why should he? His wife, teenaged daughter, and eleven-year-old son had just surprised him for his forty-fourth birthday with a Big Fun Cookie Cake, a chocolate-chip confection the size of a hubcap. His family added kisses and hugs and "You're the best daddy!" Life was good. In addition, his Christmas tree farm and school bus businesses, there in a small Virginia town, were doing well, and in the last year, he managed to diminish both his cholesterol count and his paunch through diligent exercise. One couldn't have a better September.

Sure, Cheryl, his wife, had been consumed lately with her job in D.C. for Siemens, the German technology and electronics company, but the kids continued to do well in school, and Cheryl remained upbeat with her new position. In the last year, with their extra money, they had been able to add onto their house and buy the hot tub with all the different jets they had wanted. Darryl found that to sit out under the stars and simmer in the water, a jet massaging the base of his spine, and to contemplate how small and lucky he was—well, that was what life was about.

Alone in the hot water late on his birthday afternoon, Darryl noted that the bamboo that he had planted around the propane gas tank to hide the pregnant white monster was not really doing the job. The bamboo looked stupid, like a bunch of chopsticks fronting an abandoned auto. Why did he bring in something foreign when, hell, a stand of Christmas trees would have made a better curtain?

The phone rang. He had forgotten to bring the wireless handset with him. Surely his mother or father was calling to wish him a happy birthday. With no one else home, Darryl leapt out of the water, wrapped a towel around his red suit, and dashed into the house, leaving wet footprints on the blond oak floor.

"Hello?" said Darryl, expecting a song or cheer in return.

"Darryl? It's me, Ruth—Mike's wife."

Mike was a fairly new friend. Darryl had picked Mike randomly from the "slug" line two months ago when Darryl had had a series of meetings in the city. He convinced Cheryl not to take her daily train, but rather drive in with him on I-95 each morning. However, to avoid the crush of the freeway and use the commuter lanes, dubbed the HOV lanes, they needed three or more in their car to qualify as a "high-occupancy vehicle." Because the HOV lanes were fast—and the fines were quite heavy for those caught without at least three in their car—people volunteered themselves as passengers, and a whole culture had emerged around the lanes. The volunteers became known as slugs; any suburban commuter train station had a "slug line." A slug saved money in transportation, and you, the driver, saved time.

Darryl and Cheryl had gone to the nearby train station where a man who introduced himself as Mike Freemont climbed into their car. He was a talkative, likeable fellow, versus the silent type who liked to read the paper or listen to a Walkman on the fifty-minute drive. They soon learned this gray-haired father of six had left politics, where he had been a blue-blazered consultant, to become a golf-shirted computer programmer. He, too, worked at Siemens, but Cheryl didn't know him.

"Six kids?" Cheryl asked that first morning. "Isn't that expensive in this day and age?"

"We're Catholic," said Mike.

"So are we," said Darryl, "but thanks to Vatican Two, you know, we don't feel guilty about birth control."

"My wife Ruth's from a large family, so she wanted at least six. What the heck—it's the information age. Plenty of opportunity for them to make money when they grow up." Darryl and Cheryl came to see, after they picked up Mike everyday from then on from his house, that Mike often spoke of the many opportunities in the information age.

"How are you, Ruth?" Darryl now said into the phone.

"I'm not fine," said Ruth. "A terrible situation."

"Why? What's wrong?" he asked. Cookie remnants now somersaulted in Darryl's stomach.

"Is Cheryl there right now?" she said.

"No. She's got a huge project this month, so she has to work today."

"In D.C.?"

"Yes."

"Same with Mike—even though they work in completely different divisions. I've been suspecting them for months."

"What?"

"I think they're having an affair."

Darryl could only laugh. "I'm sorry, Ruth, but that's not possible." Darryl imagined Ruth's thin body sitting in a semi-fetal position, like a question mark. She worried about such things as the trans-fatty acids in French fries and the perfume in scented soap. She had bought a radon detector for their basement and a special thousand-dollar Culligan filter unit for their kitchen tap water—all signs, in his mind, of needless fretting. "We each have kids, Ruth," Darryl said, "and we know each other all too well for them to have an affair."

"You think?" said Ruth, hopeful.

"Absolutely. First of all, Mike clearly adores you. Second, remember last week when you had us over? We were all talking about our senator, what's his name? Having sex in the elevator with his intern?"

"Billings?"

"Yeah, your husband upset my wife."

"I don't remember that."

"You were off making lemonade. Mike explained that men and women, after millions of years in the human race, were governed by different primal urges. While men have millions of sperm daily, women have only so many precious eggs and have to be selective with mates—only the top man for the job. Your husband said if you were a twenty-year-old intern, wouldn't you figure a senator—or president—was tops? Wouldn't your eggs be calling for the top guy?"

"That's stupid."

"Exactly! And my wife said that's the stupidest thing she ever heard Mike say. Did Mike's sperm shout out things?"

"She was talking about his sperm?"

"You're missing my point!" said Darryl. "If she and Mike were having an affair, would she treat him that way? Put it another way. Cheryl and I are fine. We never fight. We like each other. If she were having an affair, I'd know."

"Really?"

"Sure."

"Except Mike's become so quiet lately. He doesn't argue anymore when I ask him to do things around the house—so I think he must be feeling guilty about something."

"You feel bad because he's *not* arguing?"

"Yeah."

"Maybe he's happy, Ruth. He has his job and his family and his Budweiser—what more is there?"

"God, I hope there's something more."

Darryl then told her as gently as possible that maybe she's just depressed in general. The twins, her youngest, after all, had just entered the first grade. Maybe she was experiencing separation anxiety. Maybe she just needed a booster of some kind—like a steaming cup of hot tea or a good lobster dinner.

"You're a kind man, Darryl," she said. "Thank you. You're sensitive."

Back in the hot tub, Darryl smiled at the thought that Ruth could see his sensitivity. Cheryl accused him at times of being incapable of deep emotion, but Cheryl was wrong. He felt things. What was he supposed to do—cry to show he cared?

As Darryl lay back, staring into the afternoon sky, he wondered could Cheryl have an affair? No. She was a work junkie and too cynical to have another relationship. If she were having an affair, she'd have to schedule it. Spontaneity was not her suit.

After another few minutes, Darryl rose from the water, flesh steaming. While toweling dry, Darryl felt uneasy, much as he did a few nights earlier when he had dreamt he had to give a speech to his high school alumni association. For some reason, they were all in Hawaii at a bongo factory. He was terrified of speaking in front of the alumni and bongo workers. Also, except for a flowered lei, he was completely naked. He felt the same way now, suddenly vulnerable, wondering what if he weren't satisfying Cheryl? She seemed fine when they had sex every week or so, but did women need more sex or, as he had read on a *Vogue* cover in the grocery store last week, did he have to give more emotion? What did women want from a guy? He was doing the best emoting he could.

Darryl decided he needed to get away from such idiotic thoughts and occupy himself. His daughter had given him a video of *Dr. No* for his birthday, and it was high time he watched it.

Bond, James Bond, fell into acts of procreation like mad as he did in each Ian Fleming mystery. In this one, Bond's sperm were trying to intermingle with the eggs of a woman named Honey Ryder, played by Ursula Andress, who strode around in a bikini bottom and a white, translucent shirt. If he were Honey Ryder, Darryl thought, he'd want James Bond's sperm. Bond was the top guy. Her genes and the call of human history yearned for the top guy. That thought made Darryl wonder who was more "top"—Mike or himself? Computer programmer or entrepreneur?

Cheryl returned home just as the movie ended. She came into the living room with a small box. "I thought I'd give you one more gift," she said. "I know you loved the Skil Saw, but it just didn't seem personal enough for me."

"No, it was great," he said, sitting up and happily taking the gift. The wrapping was made from the front page of the newspaper, with a color photograph of a tornado's destruction.

"I didn't have wrapping paper at work," she explained.

Inside the small box was a cut-out paper circle divided into six pie wedges. Colors were drawn in the wedges by crayon. Green opposed red, orange opposed blue, purple opposed yellow. He frowned. He didn't understand.

"Remember, we were in the hot tub and you were saying you wished you were a painter—to capture such a landscape—minus the propane tank, of course."

"Yeah, but—"

"You said you used to love to paint but were terrible with colors. This is a color wheel."

"Huh?"

"The colors go in pairs, see." She pointed at the pairs. "The colors complete and enhance each other. If you're painting a green landscape, then you'd want to use a little red."

He gazed into her face, seeing her blue eyes watch him. He glanced back at the wheel and realized how it worked. She really must love him. He drew toward her, just wanting to kiss her. She turned her cheek as if expecting his usual peck, but he gently nudged her face back and gave a little extra. She looked at him with a bit of surprise—happily so, it seemed. He kissed her passionately, and he started to unzip her red dress on the green couch.

"No—the kids," she said.

"They're each at friends' houses tonight," he reminded her. And she relented. They made love on the floor as *Dr. No* in the VCR moved into automatic rewind.

Late in October, while she was frying pork chops, and the onions were browning, Cheryl announced to Darryl that she was pregnant. Darryl nearly dropped his glass of milk, the one of four he forced himself to drink each day. Mike's wife Ruth had told him about male osteoporosis and the need for calcium in the older man. "Pregnant. How?"

"Remember how amorous you were on the night of your birthday? You practically raped me. I didn't have time for the usual precautions."

"A baby?"

"We don't have much choice."

"But this doesn't fit our plans. You didn't want more kids. You wanted to work."

"All children should be blessed," said Cheryl, adding a tab of butter to the onions. "Mike and Ruth have six, and they're all loved."

"So you want six kids, just like Mike? Poor Ruth barely has a chance to get out of the house. Is that what you want for yourself?"

"What's wrong with you? I thought you'd be happy!"

"I'm sorry," he said. "Of course, I'm happy." And they hugged. She went back to the pork chops, and he sat down at the kitchen table where he drank his milk. Of course he should be ecstatic. He probably was. Since his birthday, however, he had spoken to Ruth a few more times about Mike. She still felt something was odd with him. She said she caught Mike whistling the other day—he never whistles.

"He's happy, for crissakes, Ruth," he'd said.

"You don't think women can sense these things, do you?"

"I don't know."

"And he's now taking his shirts to the laundry. He usually wears golf shirts," she said. "Why's he wearing buttoned shirts suddenly?"

"Winter?" Darryl offered, but he started to see her point, especially since Cheryl had once urged Darryl to dress better, saying the only way to get ahead was to get some buttoned shirts. "Trees and bus drivers don't give a shit how I dress," he had replied. "I do," she said and left it at that. But could Cheryl have an affair with Mike? No. After all, on the night of his birthday, her kisses were deep. Her sweat, her need, her love was real. Definitely real. It had to be real.

Darryl now looked at Cheryl at the stove, frying, so seemingly content. "You're not having an affair with Mike Freemont, are you?" he asked.

Her hand touched the hot pan, and she cried, "Shit!" She turned to him, angry. "Of course I'm not having an affair with Mike Freemont! Are you nuts? Look what you made me do." She sucked her hand where it was burned. "Damn it."

"I just need to know if you love me."

"Here I'm pregnant, and you wonder if I love you?"

"I know, but—"

"A new baby—all that responsibility—and you feel trapped, don't you?"

"No! I couldn't be happier. I'm a regular clam."

"You have a funny way of showing it."

"I'm sorry." He hugged her, kissed her on the cheek, and said he'd leave her alone.

"Dinner'll be in fifteen minutes," she emphasized.

"I'll tell the kids."

Weeks went by. Cheryl started to thicken with her pregnancy, but he kept getting thinner—from doubt. There was absolutely no evidence of a betrayal. Even so, he was hypersensitive to anything out of the ordinary. She changed brands of milk—why? At the movies one evening, she ordered Dots instead of her usual Red Vines. Why? The next time she had to work late, he couldn't bring himself to eat. That night, after he initiated sex, he changed his mind. He said he didn't want to hurt the baby.

"What?" she said.

"What if I poked it with my penis?

"It was never a problem with the previous children," she said.

"I'm older and wiser," he replied.

She looked at him with a frown, as if reading beyond his face. He realized then that he didn't like the idea of a creature inside watching—particularly if it wasn't his creature.

Cheryl seemed perfectly content without sex. In fact, the next day, she seemed incredibly happy. She pulled out the old crib from the garage and put it together without asking him to assist. She painted it a pretty, glossy light blue with a few orange hearts (perfect, according to his color wheel), and when he asked how she knew it'd be a boy, she told him not to be ridiculous in stereotyping color. "Girls can have blue," she said. "Color is what you make it."

All that autumn, his orange buses picked up school children with backpacks brown or blue. He had two managers for his bus business, and they kept the day-to-day operation working like a NASA mission to Mars. The schedules were met, engines were tuned, and the occasional graffiti was removed from the back of seats. Darryl arranged it so that he wasn't really needed there. He'd oversee the books, but he preferred working his pines. In September, he had helped cut down the dead trees, which they burned, as well as cut down boundary trees for sunlight. A week before Thanksgiving, after all the deciduous leaves had fallen and browned like burnt caramel, he went into one of his fields to tag which Christmas trees should be cut. The first ones were always the spruce. Then came the Fraser, Douglas, Virginia Pines, and Concolor Firs. He preferred the spruce, which had the strongest branches, ideal for holding ornaments.

Evergreens, he realized, seemed to be like wives: they didn't look any different, yet, at the end of the summer, they seemed somehow taller and surer and totally mysterious. He and his crew would shape the trees during the summer, but could one ever shape a wife? Now, this time of year, the trees didn't need him and neither did his bus business. Did his wife? Did he have a purpose for anyone or anything? He had a big house, good income, amenable children, and yet he felt as useful as a bailing bucket on the Titanic.

After such thoughts one crisp November day, Darryl headed for Ruth's, then and there. As he approached her house, the morning felt pale, and the leafless trees in the surrounding woods looked like bones against a gray sheet. As usual, Ruth welcomed him and even knew how he liked his coffee—with milk and two packets of sugar. When Darryl told her of Cheryl's blossoming condition, he stopped. Ruth's eyebrows went up, expecting him to say more.

"The thing is," he said, "This iffiness is killing me. Look at me. I've lost twenty pounds because I can't eat well anymore. Doubt is not a good feeling to have."

"It's all my fault. I feel like throwing up," said Ruth.

"Maybe we could throw up together."

They hugged each other. Darryl could feel tears coming to his eyes, which he commanded to stop. What was he going to do next, blubber? He was falling apart. He pulled away, turned his face so she couldn't see.

"How can people have affairs?" he said. "Do they like messing up their lives and others?"

"I don't know."

"I just try to live life simply, you know? Be a good person."

"Yes, yes."

"I'd give anything to know the real truth."

They hugged each other, and, without thinking, started kissing, quite passionately. He felt her tongue and returned her urgency. She smelled so much different than Cheryl, a wonderful perfume in place of Cheryl's more talcum smell— the reality of that made him quiver. Ruth's hand stroked the back of his head, slithered into his hair sensuously. Her other bare hand was under the back of his shirt, and he could sense the press of her breasts against his chest. He moved his own hands under her shirt, and her skin felt so warm and smooth, he wanted to feel and see more.

He and Ruth fell to the floor. He was on top of her, and though they were still clothed, he felt her hips thrust forward with his. The hot iron of guilt sizzled its way into him, however, and Darryl pushed himself off. "I love Cheryl," he said.

"And I love Mike."

With awkwardness and a patting of their clothes, they stood. Ruth's expression, though, paralleled that of a child forced to a summer camp she didn't want to attend. He felt his knees were going to buckle once more. But were his feelings for her a mistake? "We just like each other, you and I. Nothing wrong with that," he said.

She touched his arm lightly. "It's okay."

"Really?"

"We've both been under a lot of pressure."

"All I know is that when I was twelve, things were easier," he said. "I could go out and order a chocolate malt at the drugstore fountain, and everything would be fine."

"Yes," she added. "The TV wasn't trumpeting our leader's indiscretions and breaking our trust in everything. Trust is important."

"And forty five cents was all it cost at the Rexall," said Darryl.

"For trust?"

"No! A chocolate malt."

"Oh. I loved those things."

"Let's get one," Darryl said, looking into her green eyes.

Ruth at first seemed to think that getting a malt was an odd thing to do, but Darryl said that they deserved at least something good in their lives. If chocolate malts, even at four dollars each, did it, then it was worth it. "I mean," he said, "we don't do drugs, we're not having an affair, and we're good people. So I figure we should grab all the innocent, immediate gratification we can get."

As they discussed possible places that served chocolate malts, he discovered the drink was nearly extinct. Within a short drive, there were three Seven-Eleven stores, a WalMart, and the Golden Corral Buffet. No place featured malts.

"The only place I know for sure that makes good old-fashioned malts is in Union Station in D.C." Darryl said.

"We can't go all the way in to D.C. just for a malt."

"Why not? Let's be spontaneous! The HOV lanes don't require slugs this time of day. We can get downtown and back before your kids are home from school. For the very reason it feels stupid, we should do it. We deserve it."

So they did. With Darryl the passenger, Ruth drove her Volvo station wagon at high speeds down the HOV lane, her window recklessly open, wind whistling past her ear like a lover saying hello.

Luck was with them. One street before Union Station, a car pulled out from a meter, and Ruth pulled into the space. Darryl had quarters in his pocket, but when he went to put them into the meter, he saw that nearly two hours were left on the timer.

"Are you magical or what?" Darryl said.

Ruth smiled and said, "I'm just a mom." She kept pace with Darryl as they stepped toward the grand, white granite building.

"You're a good person, Ruth. Good people are rewarded."

"With what? A trip to Vegas and a Winnebago?"

"I'm serious."

"I know."

"I'm saying—" He paused to figure out what he was saying. "I refuse to believe that you and I deserve what we've been going through. We're good people. There's got to be some goodness in the end. I know it."

As he looked to check for traffic before crossing the street, he realized that Cheryl worked only about eight blocks from the station on Pennsylvania Avenue. "Siemens is close," he said without thinking.

"You want to go there?"

"No. I didn't mean that."

"There I go inferring again."

The thing was, the thought indeed had popped into his head: should they go there? No. He was here to enjoy an innocent adventure with Ruth.

A traffic cop blew his whistle, and cars came to a halt. Darryl looked at the man briefly, wondering if the whistle was a sign—but why would it be? Darryl and Ruth stepped through the door, the portal of the station.

The bright, pearl-white luster of the curved ceiling high above reminded Darryl of the inside of an oyster shell, which reminded him of Ruth's thigh, which made him think of sex. Sex came to mind, too, from the bubbling of the nearby water fountain, the plunk of an old man's cane on the marble, the flash of Ruth's hand as she stepped forward. Sex, sex, sex. But he should control himself. Control, control, control.

"I haven't been here since I don't know when," Ruth said.

"At the time it was built," said Darryl, "it was the largest railway station in the world."

She nodded and smiled, as if he'd been flirting.

They walked. As he strode in harmony with Ruth's footsteps, a sense of awe welled up in him. It reminded him of when he was a kid, standing at the start of a baseball game. Fifty thousand people could stand in unison and sing the National Anthem in front of grass so green and men in uniforms so white, and this moment seemed similarly right and innocent. They should be proudly hailing.

They passed small restaurants, a postcard shop, and a woman in a long, blue gown who played on a violin in a corner, and her music, loud and yearning, carried Darryl and Ruth down the concourse. He could smell hot Italian food and the earthiness of a leather shop.

"Ah," said Darryl, "This is the place," and he pointed to an ice cream shop whose white wrought-iron tables and chairs reminded him of an old-fashioned confectionery. He motioned for her to sit. "Two chocolate malts coming up," he said.

She reached for her purse, but he waved it off, saying, "Don't be silly."

When Darryl returned with their malts in tall, cone-shaped glasses, he paused as he observed Ruth gazing at the people walking by. She appeared in awe, as if she had just risen from a coma. When her gaze came to Darryl and the creamy concoctions, she smiled widely, as if he were the main reason why she was now conscious. He felt his blood pound harder. He felt himself becoming erect. How embarrassing. He had to sit down quickly, hoping she hadn't noticed. He couldn't remember a single time as an adult having an erection in public. What's going on? Was this love? If so, what had been all the feelings he had had with Cheryl?

He looked more closely at Ruth, at the very lips he had kissed, and he felt as if the English language had then evaporated, that everything he had understood was wrong. Purple was red. Yellow was orange. Everything felt so strange lately, strange now, strange this second. Was love not a choice? But choosing Ruth could bring so much pain.

Ruth continued to gaze at his face, too, but when she sipped her malt, she looked back at the people walking by. He studied her studying, and she was beautiful. She had naturally wavy auburn hair that nearly reached her shoulders, ears that held delicate loops of gold, and a small nose that could have been carved by an artisan with an Italian-sounding wine name such as Chianti.

"Seems like there're two kinds of people in this world," she said.

"What do you mean?"

"First, there are the desensitized." She pointed to a glum couple in gray. The man, in a business suit, walked a step or two ahead of a woman, probably his wife, who had good posture, kept a blank face and did not glance at her surroundings at all. They moved like stonemasons toward the same old quarry.

"...And then there are the curious." She pointed to a neat, longhaired man in his thirties walking mostly backwards, talking animatedly with a blond-haired woman perhaps ten years his senior. The woman spoke just as eagerly back, using her hands expressively. Maybe they were Italians. Maybe they were artisans.

"The desensitized and the curious? How do you come up with such things?" he said.

She laughed, bringing up a hand to cover her mouth. He gently touched her hand, stopping it.

"You have a lovely smile. Don't cover it."

She brought her hands down and clasped them, looking down at them. He leaned over to look up into her eyes. She moved her face down. They kissed. He felt her tongue, her need, both of which matched his. When he opened his eyes a dozen heartbeats later, his lips still pressed against Ruth, he saw a couple out in the hallway staring at them. It was Cheryl and Mike. They appeared dumbfounded.

Ruth now saw them, too, and stood so fast, her chair fell over, banging onto the tile. "What are you doing here?" she gasped.

"We might ask you the same thing." Then he laughed. "We work near here. And you?"

Cheryl said, "And to think we were worried about you two."

Crying instantly, Ruth ran out of the shop, turning a sharp left, leaving Darryl to stare at one thing: the clasped hands of his wife and Mike. Now he knew: they were lovers.

Darryl felt his throat constrict, and if he wanted to scream, he could not do so. He desperately looked for Ruth. She was gone. Darryl fell to his knees. His stomach wrenched. He promptly lost his chocolate malt, spilling onto the white tile. The brown colors reminded him of a Big Fun Cookie Cake, which he never had again.

# The Fundamentals Of Nuclear Dating

The light went green at the intersection near Starbucks and Radio Shack. The latter store was closed for the holiday, and the other featured people out in the whistle-clean Culver City sky at round tables and dressed in their Easter best, laughing, touching, and slugging down Macchiatos and Caramel Frappuccinos. Jules accelerated, smiling.

At the sound of the screeching tires, Jules glanced to his left to see an SUV the size of a giant black redwood headed smack at him. Jules instinctively stepped on the brakes. Why? To have the SUV slam into him more cleanly? To give the café goers something to talk about that night? He could see the other driver grimace and crank his steering wheel hard. Hard. Harder. Time was a Speedo elastic band about to snap. Jules flashed on his son, Eric, red hair from a bottle, a key-chain earring, and an attitude that shouted help. How would Eric react to a flattened father? The two-ton vehicle was now moving sideways toward Jules. Was it going to flip? Was he going to be a pancake? Why now?

The SUV shimmied to a stop, parallel to Jules's white Toyota Corolla, the only thing he owned free and clear after his marriage of fifteen years. Five inches separated the two cars. The other driver was shaking. Jules was shaking. People at the Starbucks were not shaking but rather standing in awe, witnesses to an Easter miracle. Rebirth, someone's lips may have formed. The light was still green. Jules pressed the accelerator again.

He was at Ralphs grocery store in another minute, but now he rethought his mission. After a series of five awkward dates thanks to Match.com, Jules had spoken to his cousin in New York who told him if he was serious about finding someone new, go daily to Ralphs. Don't buy food for the refrigerator, but, rather, go to the grocery store everyday, noonish on weekends and 5:30 on weekdays, to buy only a one-day supply of food. In that way he'd have the best chance to run into good working women. The cheese section was best. Working women liked cheese.

Going to Ralphs daily had sounded stupid, but Gwen, his next date, had appeared near the Camembert. Alas, over a Mocha Valencia, he discovered that Gwen, a 32-year-old librarian, hated house cleaning, and her apartment was always a mess. "I'm orderly all day long, so I can't stand to be neat at night," she said as if it were a casual, innocuous fact like mauve was her favorite color for a bathroom. Jules, however, instantly crossed her name off his mental list. He would not make the mistake again of living with someone messy.

He had become very matter-of-fact after his divorce and after his Match.com dates. He figured out a few things: Do not date 1) anyone who hated men in general or was clinically depressed; 2) anyone who dog-eared her weekly copy of *TV Guide*; 3) anyone who kept a loaded shotgun under her bed; 4) anyone who kept a small pyramid over her birth control pills in the bathroom or believed in the positive health effects of red light bulbs; 5) anyone who thought the Klu Klux Klan was misunderstood; 6) anyone who didn't have a child because she would not understand his; 7) anyone who traveled a lot, or had no pets, as this meant she did not want to be tied down or take responsibility; 8) anyone who talked at length about Mrs. Healy, who seemed to be a neighbor but turned out to be one of several dolls she still collected, and 9) anyone who wrote on Match.com that she was bright, beautiful, and loved to listen. It really meant she never went to college, thought beauty was in the eye of the surgeon, and loved to talk at length about Mrs. Healy.

Jules also had some positive rules. Do date someone with a young child, as she will understand the juggling that is required in joint custody. Do date someone who looks sexy; chemistry is half of everything. Cleanliness is the other half. Do date someone with a sense of humor, especially if she liked the old movie *Harold and Maude*.

This meant it was back to Ralphs. Except no more after this, Jules decided. He was going to buy food for a month. The universe—or at least the SUV—told him his luck was running out. Stay home or be struck by lightning.

Jules stepped into the store and noted the smell of fresh coffee and saw a new addition to the place: a Starbucks stand. It hadn't been there yesterday. Were Starbucks like seeds in the wind? Such a fast change threw him off his stride. So did the tall, auburn-haired woman nearby. A two-year-old girl with the same-colored hair, but curly, sat in the woman's shopping basket. "Man, Momma," the girl said and pointed to Jules. The woman turned, Jules paused in the turnstile, and when the woman smiled, so did he. He noticed no wedding ring.

The woman leaned close to the girl. "Yes, that's a man."

"Her hair sticks up," said the essence of cuteness, looking at Jules.

"*His* hair sticks up," said the girl's mother, who then turned to Jules. "I'm sorry. She's learning the difference between the sexes."

"No bother," said Jules. "I'm still learning, and I haven't gotten very far."

The woman laughed.

"*His* hair sticks up," said the little girl.

"Yes, *his*," said the mother, and she leaned in closer to whisper, "but it's not nice to point out defects." Oh great, Jules thought to himself: his defects show already.

To turn his face away quickly, Jules strode up to the Starbucks' counter. "I'll have a tall whatever the flavor of the day is," said Jules to the aproned Starbucks server, a blond high school girl.

"Sumatra," said the girl.

Kama Sumatra, Jules thought, sex these days flashing on his mind like a bulb in a movie marquee. He hadn't had any sex for several months, and he wondered if he were no different than salmon, swimming up the river to Ralphs. His genes put him in jeans and had him troll among wedges of cultured milk products to woo the way pilots needed planes or Rustoleum needed rust. Who would want him: awkward, so damn needy, and with a cowlick?

"Yes, that will be good," said Jules. "A tall Sumatran." This world kept him guessing, a world where tall was really short, and Sumatra didn't refer to an Indonesian woman in a 19th century oil painting, but to a bean. How absurd, he thought, of how he was even there at that moment. You were just around for a series of coincidences and then you died.

Jules' face wasn't hidden for long, as the mother moved her cart around the corner, interested in a one-pound vacuum-packed bag of House Blend—or so it seemed. Was she perhaps interested in him? The little girl farted, and the mother looked at the girl quizzically. The girl then said, "Him did it," pointing again to Jules.

"No," said the mother, "*He* did it."

"I didn't!" Jules protested. "I think maybe your daughter did or—" He looked at the server.

"*I* didn't do it," said the high school girl.

The woman was laughing now, covering her mouth. "I'm sorry," she said. "Helen always blames someone else. Usually it's our dog, a little Chihuahua. I think she got it from a rerun of *Seinfeld*."

"You can get dogs from *Seinfeld*?" said Jules.

The woman, concerned, said, "No, I meant—"

"I'm kidding," said Jules, and the woman laughed anew.

"That's a dollar fifty," said the server, shoving the coffee toward Jules.

"Have you ever seen *Harold and Maude*?" Jules impulsively asked.

"Love it," said the woman. "That and *Annie Hall*. Why?"

"*Annie Hall*'s fabulous, too."

What Jules had learned already about this woman before him was 1) he loved auburn hair; 2) he loved her smile and her tall stature; 3) she had a dog, a good thing; 4) she also had a young daughter and responsibly taught the girl personal pronouns; 5) there was chemistry.

"Are you looking for a housekeeper?" Jules blurted.

"No," she said, and frowned, looking at him anew. "I keep a very clean house, thank you." She was turning away again.

"I'm sorry, I ask silly things when I'm nervous. I'm not a housekeeper—my friend is. I'm a graphic designer. I meant to ask would you like a cup of coffee?"

The woman held up her cup. "I've already got some."

Damn the Starbucks people—they were ruining the ecology of grocery store dating. "Right," said Jules. And Jules was losing the moment. She was giving him the nice-to-meet-you nod and was turning, headed for the Lays Potato Chip two-for-one display.

Help. No solution came to his mind. The frozen Breyers ice cream on sale nearby gave a glacial look. Marie Callender's frozen pot pies for one said saying they'd be sharing many evenings together. There was no destiny. He had not been saved to meet this woman and her daughter.

He sucked in his cheeks as was his bad habit when he was saddened, which gave him a chipmunk face. Little Helen, who was departing but observing Jules, mimicked him and laughed. Oh yeah? He pulled his eyes and cheeks together to make a funny look, and the little girl did that, too. The mother saw her daughter, frowned, turned and saw Jules, and looked impressed, as if Jules had just unlocked Fort Knox.

"Camilla," she said, striding over and reaching out her hand. *Her* hand.

"Jules." He zipped out his hand.

"I normally don't do this," she said boldly, "But would you like to meet for a drink later? I can get a friend to baby-sit."

And his coffee, with its random bean beginnings, steamed in glee.

# Dear Ma

*B* lue eagles glide down and race together across the sand back and forth from the waves, and those skinny young men in Mexico jump into the air and screech in delight. The arms of the bay rise and the water flashes like watch bands, don't fall, don't fall, how glorious, let's do it. Water's warm. Warm. What?

"Some beets, Dear Ma?"

Dear Ma considered the blue eyes of the young woman. Like the sky.

"I think you hear me, don't you?"

"Beets?" She looked down. "Oh."

"Can you understand me? What I'm saying?"

"Yes," she said with a nod.

The young woman's high-cheekboned face, smooth and Scandinavian, gleamed like new fruit. She hugged Dear Ma around the shoulders. "You're back!"

"Sounds like I was at it a while." She glanced around her salmon-colored bedroom, a room her husband always considered pink.

"Two days."

"A long one."

"Yes."

"Did Teddy call the doctor?"

"Max did. He—"

"My son worries too much."

"I was worried! You didn't eat. You'd keep your eyes shut and say things I couldn't understand. The doctor gave you some glucose, and I was to give you more."

"Thank you, Pia. Teddy gone?" Pia nodded. Dear Ma yanked the blanket out from the spokes in her wheelchair—a device she needed only within the last year—and tucked the spread tighter around her legs. "I was back in Mexico with Max and Teddy, and I was trying to talk them into strapping on a parachute. You should have seen their expressions! Max wanted it so, but Teddy—"

"Skydiving? I would never—"

"No no. On almost any beach down there you can find some enterprising boys who've connected a parachute to the back of a motorboat. You float all over the bay like a whisper. Teddy didn't like the idea."

"He probably couldn't do it in a coat and tie," said Pia.

Dear Ma laughed at the implication. She wheeled herself out from behind the card table, a setup that allowed her to eat in her bedroom, and leaned forward as if telling a secret. "We once had a fire in the laundry room. I yelled to the kids to grab their robes, run outside! The fire department thundered here in minutes, and we all stood outside like toy soldiers, when I noticed my husband missing. I ran back in. There's Teddy in the bathroom adjusting his tie. Goddamn it, I said, get outside! But he told me, 'Jen, we're far from the flames, and I need to look proper. The firemen have their uniform, and so do I.'"

Pia laughed but turned away. "An unusual man," she said.

"A true Virgo. To this day, before he goes to bed, he chooses what he'll wear the next day and hangs it in the bathroom. Where is Teddy, anyway?"

"The post office."

"Mailing checks for bills, no doubt. Here I am, hardly cognizant half the time, and he treats me as if I'm the woman he married."

Pia set a plate of food in front of her.

Dear Ma glared at the beets. "I detest any vegetable that's redder than my lipstick."

"You've got to get stronger," Pia said, and she served one more beet from a silver tray. The crimson juice oozed around the mashed potatoes.

"Beets will give me hemorrhoids."

"Come now."

"They will. They're filled with iron. And because I sit all day, the iron will zip right to my derrière."

"What would you like instead?"

"An artichoke."

Pia nodded as if that were not difficult. Dear Ma stared at the young woman, then quickly looked about the room. Something was out of balance here. Despite day-to-day changes, a room has a certain harmony to it, like a garden. Teddy's open, half-read mystery story rested next to her chaise longue, his socks lay under his twin bed, and her desk appeared quite tidy with no papers showing. None of these things seemed out of place. It was Pia's "yes."

"An artichoke'll take an hour to cook," Dear Ma said slowly.

"That's all right."

There had to be something new and wrong with her condition that Pia wasn't telling her. Dear Ma felt a fist rise in her stomach, a hand yank on her insides.

"Dear Ma!" Pia rushed over. Dear Ma's eyes fluttered and her arms shook. "Stop," Pia shouted. "Focus on my face!" Too late.

*I don't love him I just can't. Hand hits table and spoons dance like leaves Paris in the spring I won't marry him.*

"Jeannine, you're being ridiculous. Gerald has a future, and talk about a fine family, you can't get more respect than the Marklethiels. You'll live in Kenwood," her mother said. They sat at a white round table at an outdoor café. A new 1920 Model-T was trying to park as a horse-drawn carriage swept past it.

Jeannine purposely paused, not only for effect, but also to pull in the rich, earthy smells of her café au lait. She drank it too quickly. The coffee burnt her tongue, but she didn't let her mother take note. Instead, she gathered the many folds of her skirt and swung them and herself around so she faced the Champs Elysee.

"Jeannine, sometimes you can be so theatrical." Her mother, resplendent in a lacy, yet stiffly pressed blouse and a long skirt, nodded to the mustached waiter for the bill. "Honestly, how can we shop for your trousseau if you're not going to marry the man? I'm sorry, but at this point you have no say in the matter."

"I can't. I don't love him."

"Then why're we here? Why did you come?"

"I was tricked."

Her mother slapped the table and was going to say something when Jeannine continued: "Do you think I had any chance with Father and the Marklethiels pushing so hard?"

"What's wrong with Gerald?"

"First, I don't think he has a sense of humor. Second, he always calls me Sis, and if he says it one more time, I'm going to bash him. Third, Gerald T. Marklethiel, is named Gerald T. Marklethiel. And fourth, he affects a Boston accent that simply nauseates me!"

"He's from Boston!"

Jeannine tilted her head back and became her fiancé. "Shall we mota ova to the club? Ah, Mrs. Pinopscott, what a jaunty muffla you ah spahting."

Her mother, despite herself, released a smile.

"And Mrs. Rose, I shall have Sis—I mean Jahnine—home at the appointed owwa. And may I say, you have the same beautiful eyes as your lovely daughtah."

"I do?"

"Ah, Mrs. Rose, they spahcle with vibrance."

The two women laughed and held each other.

"But most of all," said Jeannine, taking advantage of the moment, "I can't marry that man because he's not part of my soul. When I saw the couples walking in the Tuilleries last night, I knew then: nothing's in me for him. If and when I marry, it'll be to someone who's handsome, witty, extremely sharp. He'll know how to ride horses and laugh and stay calm and listen and maybe fence."

"Anything else?"

"He won't make the wrong comments at the wrong time. We'll be like two matches who always burn for each other."

"Darling, there's no such person in the universe."

"I have to think so—otherwise I may as well marry anyone. Even Gerald T. Marklethiel."

"Exactly."

"Forget it."

"Jeannine, I should've never let you go to Bryn Mawr."

"Mother, I have my beliefs."

Her mother shook her head and buttered a croissant. "I know Gerald," she stressed. "He's a very sweet man. Athletic. Intelligent. Sensitive. I know you'll love him."

"The way he looks at me so lovingly gives me the willies."

"Everything is set. You'll marry Gerald."

*Sit here Jeannine next to Teddy. Thank you I liked Paris very much, I finished it all and we'll see how it works. Butter?*

A moon face drooled. Baby Jake's eyes wandered to the wall.

"Say Hi to your great granny, Jake. We call her Dear Ma. Come on, wave hello." David, her twenty-five-year-old grandchild, tall as a telephone pole, took Jake's little hand and waved it at Dear Ma while David's short wife Sandra wiped the wire of spittle that led from Jake's mouth to Dear Ma's knee.

"Jake apologizes, Dear Ma," Sandra said.

Dear Ma raised her head for the first time in four days. Pia, embroidering yellow mums onto a pillow, moved forward, her senses tuning in. "Are you—can you see me?"

"Yes."

"It's me, David," said David.

Dear Ma didn't say anything more. She locked onto the baby's eyes, and the baby pushed back behind its mask and declared *I have the years and you haven't but you can breathe me in if you want to.*

Pia knelt next to Dear Ma, took her hand. "David here was just telling us that Jake's starting to stand. He can almost walk."

Have I fallen onto a dock? Why are they glaring their stares into me? I'm not drowning.

"Should I get Max, Dear Ma?"

Dear Ma felt her own face. She remembered. This is the place where things were happening now. Why was she getting worse?

"I think she's saying something," said Pia.

"What?" asked Sandra.

"Teddy," said Dear Ma.

"Teddy, over here!" cried Jeannine from the shore. 1944.

As if a starting gun had gone off, the broad-shouldered man bolted up from his prone position on the beach, and immediately he rose and sprinted in the direction of the water. His feet tore into the hot beach, producing a swooshing sound. Shots of sand arched behind him. Jeannine watched her husband in motion as he ran toward the water, not to her. He looked wonderful—almost ageless. He didn't see her sitting near the shore to his right. When he did, he stopped abruptly. "Jen, I thought you were drowning."

"I've found a treasure in the sky," she said. "It's El Dorado!"

"Ma, where!" shouted Max, a bronze stick who leaped out of his sand pit faster than any nine-year-old in Mexico.

Only Max had joined them on this trip, as his older sisters were already out of the house, either in college or married.

"Out in the bay. Look," Jeannine said. The wind blew some of her shoulder-length hair across her eyes. She pulled the hair away as she pointed.

"I don't see it," said Max, legging past his father. "Where?"

Teddy slapped the sand off his well-muscled body and moved his mouth as if exaggerating the hint of saltiness that he tasted from the air. He looked to the red bubble tied to the speedboat. "Jen, that's a parachute."

"Isn't it something! We can ride it."

"No we can't."

"Please, Pop," shouted Max.

"I'm not Pop, I'm Father. And she's your Mother, not Ma. You've been seeing too many Shirley Temple movies."

"Well?" said Jeannine.

"Absolutely, positively not," said Teddy. "I've only got a week's leave. I'm not about to see my family gadding about in the sky."

"Oh, Teddy."

"I worry enough as is about you. You want to give me nightmares when I'm back at sea?"

The speedboat approached but soon turned sharply away. "Sure would be fun," said Max, watching.

"High tide's coming soon, Max," said Teddy. "And you haven't built the walls to your sand castle yet."

"The dungeon's not done!"

"Better hurry."

The boy, instantly charged, scooted off. Jeannine moved closer to Teddy. He took her around the waist. She curled her fingers softly into his stomach, his damp-from-sweat skin. Through the scent of aftershave, she smelled a wonderful muskiness, reminding her of their morning's lovemaking—far better than any six months of letters. She looked up into her husband's blue eyes.

He opened his mouth as if to say something, but did not. Instead, he moved in. They kissed. When they pulled apart, he tucked a strand of her brown hair around her ear. "I love you," he said.

She drew her finger along his neck up to his mouth. "Even if I said I'd still like to go up?"

He shook his head, growing a grin. "Sometimes I can't believe you! But yes, I love you even if you want to grab onto that fool parachute."

He hugged her. And then looked at the boat again.

Thirty minutes later, Jeannine, aloft, could barely hear the drone of the motor below her. Teddy and Max—in the boat—waved, and she waved back. The rope drew up from them and, like an electric wire plugging her into the wind, pulled her along.

"Excelsior!" she screamed. "Teddy, Max, you'll have to try this!" She imagined Max hearing her and pointing and jumping.

There was a slight jerk.

It took her a moment to realize she was going down while the boat was going out. The rope had snapped. This wasn't supposed to happen. Was it? She could see the frantic dot of Teddy racing to the two T-shirted spots at the wheel. The bay came closer, closer, and she looked up. The boat curved back toward her. Just before her plunge.

Jeannine knifed down and down into the sea, and she hoped she'd stop soon because she didn't have that much breath left, and she opened her eyes and saw strings of bubbles rubbing past so she closed her eyes and the rope curled at her legs while the warm water wound around her.

Her stomach clutched, such a vile taste. Acid. Salt. And she wrenched.

A voice. A soft, concerned sound.

"Teddy?"

"Yes." She focused. Water danced on his forehead in the sunlight. She lay at the bottom of the boat, bouncing on the waves at full speed. Max stuck his face in and smiled, and a

Mexican boy kept saying, "La cuerda fue nueva," displaying the break in the frayed rope.

"Ma, it's me, Max. Pop dove in and got you!"

She looked up to her husband and saw his wet hair and trembling face. "Jen, thank God you're alive!" Teddy held her, his skin with her skin. His hug felt warm, warm as if he'd never leave.

Max stood before her, not a little boy, but a tall thin man in a white suit. Looked like a cigarette ad.

"Ma, it's me. Are you okay? The doctor says you're all right. Heart like a teenager. Can you hear me?"

"You always built the biggest sand castles. Remember that time in Mexico?"

"I know, Ma, but that's not the point. You're phasing out on me."

"Phasing out?" She looked about the room. Her bed was unmade, Teddy's book was closed, and Pia was on the phone, probably to her boyfriend.

"Yes, sleeping in your chair. You were never a sleeper."

She straightened. "You're right. I wasn't a sleeper." She stared at her aging son. "I'd like coffee."

"You know you can't have that." He leaned in. "But how about if I sneak you some coffee ice cream?"

"You've always been a charmer."

His face brightened. "You're right."

"Where's Teddy?"

"He's off. Post Office I think."

"He's writing a lot of letters lately."

"What?" He looked to Pia who, listening in, gestured back to him. "Oh, that was days ago. Now he's probably paying a bill. If you stay awake, you'll see him."

"Is he paying the taxes? Before you said he was working on the taxes."

"That was last month, and we got an accountant for that."

"Last month?" She stared at her son, at his patient, paternal look. It was as if he were humoring her. "You think of me as helpless."

"I didn't say—"

"I may be in a wheel chair, and I may 'phase out' occasionally, but I'm not helpless."

"No, you're getting better, stronger. Maybe we can take a trip soon."

"I feel grimy. I want to wash my face."

"Paris, we can go to Paris—you went there once, right?"

Max reached for her chair, but she slapped him away. "I can wheel myself." She grabbed the rubbered wheels and shoved.

"Let me help you." Max adjusted the blanket in her lap, then pushed her through the doorway and up to the sink. Her legs fit underneath the sink and her chin barely cleared the rim. Dear Ma was too low in the chair to see her face in the mirror, but she could see Max's. It looked unbalanced. His hair was parted on the wrong side, and his lips and eyebrows seemed thicker on one side than the other. "Contrary" was the word she thought.

"Let me get you a fresh bar of soap," Max said.

She saw in the mirror.

"And a washrag? You like washrags, don't you?"

She was transfixed by the mirror, for she saw in the mirror, backwards in the mirror, marked by the mirror, Teddy's clothes on a hanger on a hook on the door.

"Ma, what is it? I thought you wanted to wash your face?" Max pulled his head down next to hers and saw what she saw.

She pushed out from the sink and stared into her son's eyes. "Why didn't you tell me?"

He saw that she saw the clothes. "It's cold out there today—he's wearing different stuff, besides galoshes and things."

"No underwear? No tie? Even if he were sick, he'd insist you bring him clothes."

Max, head down, picked at a hangnail on his thumb as if that'd give reason for silence. He had had the same hang-dog posture as a child. "It happened a couple of days ago, actually."

"He died?"

He nodded. "Peacefully. In his sleep."

"And you weren't going to tell me? You kept planning to say he was at the post office?"

"You're in and out so much, we didn't know how it'd affect you. We were afraid you might never come back."

"Don't you think I deserved to know?" To breathe felt like swallowing foam. Max became a blur. She tried to steady herself, but the momentum carried her, and she tumbled toward the floor. Max reacted, but too late. She broke her own fall. Curling into a ball, she cried.

"Ma, I'm sorry." His fingers were delicate on her shoulders—he didn't know how to touch her. When she stopped, Max lifted her back into the chair.

"Ma?"

"Yes?"

"He always loved you."

She nodded. "I wonder if he was dreaming."

"What do you mean?"

"I'm fine," she said. "Take me back into the other room."

Max did so. He held her hands for the next hour and spoke of taking her away once she got better. "What do you think of that?" he said.

"Yes," said Dear Ma.


*Un autre café, s'il vous plaît. Je vous en prie.*

Jeannine purposely paused, not only for effect, but also to smell the roast in her café au lait. She gathered the many folds of her skirt and swung them and herself around so she faced the Champs Elysee.

"Everything is set, you'll marry Gerald."

"I feel... hollow, like my voice and my thoughts have separated."

"I'm not saying you *have* to marry him, but everything is set."

Jeannine looked down and shook her head slightly, as if she were a trapeze artist having doubts.

"Why did you go out with Gerald so often? Don't you like him?"

"I like his middle name better than his first."

"Middle? *Theo*dore? Are we going to buy your trousseau today or not? Are you going to marry him?" Jeannine said nothing, so her mother continued, "Shall we finish all the shopping? If you're scared of marriage, everyone gets nervous. You'll see how it works. Marriage is quite wonderful."

Jeannine paused and watched two red birds glide down from a wire. They landed on the ground two tables over.

"He prefers to be called Teddy," Jeannine said. "Yes, I'll marry Teddy."

Photo by Daniel Will-Harris

## About the Author

Christopher Meeks has had stories published in several literary journals including *Rosebud*, *Clackamas Literary Review*, and the *Santa Barbara Review*, among others. He's published two collections of short fiction, the one in your hands and *Months and Seasons*. Two of his novels are upcoming, *The Brightest Moon of the Century* and *The Laughter and Sadness of Sex*.

Mr. Meeks has had three full-length plays mounted in Los Angeles, published four children's books, reviewed theatre for seven years for *Daily Variety*, has had two screenplays optioned and another win the Donald Davis Dramatic Writing Award; he also teaches creative writing at USC's Master of Professional Writing Program and, at various times, at UCLA Extension, CalArts, Santa Monica College, and the Art Center College of Design. His column about writing can be viewed on the Internet at www.efuse.com (click on "Design" and scroll down to "Columnists"). Visit his website at:

## www.ChrisMeeks.com

www.ingramcontent.com/pod-product-compliance
Lightning Source LLC
Chambersburg PA
CBHW031605260626
47154CB00020B/1619